evergreen
tales of winter shadows

Edited by

River Eno

& LCW Allingham

Speculation Publications

Evergreen

ISBN-13: 979-8-9918553-0-3

Executive Editor: River Eno
Editor: LCW Allingham
Assistant Editor : Susan Tulio

Reprinted Work:
"The Lamplighter's Daughter" by Anne Karppinen,
Wyldblood Press, 2021

Cover Art: LCW Allingham
Book Design and Layout: LCW Allingham
Copyright © 2024 Speculation Publications LLC

Vectors and Art: Vecteezy/Valentina Sova
Fonts: Cardinal, Book Antiquita

Published by Speculation Publications
No part of this book was created by AI

For More Information go to www.speculationpub.com

To the darkness

To the grief

To the shadowed places we must pass through to find sunshine again

Table of Contents

Foreword

Psychoanalyst Carl Jung called it the shadow-self. The parts of us we keep hidden, the parts of us touched by trauma or emotions that we cannot process easily. He believed it is a counterweight to the persona we put forward every day, and an integral part of who we are.

Though sometimes difficult to acknowledge, shadows are a part of our experience, and they seek validation. Our understanding of the world, and within that, our place in it, comes from the full range of our emotions. And while digging deep into the pains that plague us can be exhausting, it can also be invigorating. Acceptance brings transformation and growth.

The long, dark nights of winter—after the unrelenting heat of summer's sunny days—seem almost created for this reflection. The inky star-filled skies we ruminate under. The blazing fires we sit at in contemplation and wonder. And the bitter nights we huddle inside, reading ourselves to different worlds and realities.

The enchanting stories and poems of Evergreen reflect the introspection of the darker season. In Jan Cronus's "His Return," Christina Roldan's "The Whispers of Woods," and Maddox Emory Arnold's "What We Buried Here," grief is explored in its complexity.

Anne Karppinen shows us a young woman yearning to grow beyond her life in "The Lamplighter's Daughter." Jordan King-Lacroix weaves a tale of grace in the shadow of sacrifice in "The Unwatched Hour." And Enid Paige envisions a whole new and wonderful world in "The Wishes of Eirlys."

This journey through winter, illustrated in "The End of our Dark" is a long one full of changes. Happiness ebbs and flows as does sadness, anger and grief; showing us all emotions are transient. They're meant to touch us as they move through us, and if our goal is to be balanced, we wouldn't want it any other way.

If we can show understanding to others for their choices, as Veikko's village does for him in "The Hunting of Tulikettu," surely, we can turn that empathy inward, to live in a world where forgiving yourself is as common a notion as forgiving others. Where peace is as inevitable as the return of warmer days, as illustrated in "March."

The soulful beauty of the stories and poems of Evergreen will captivate and charm you on a cold winter's night. Get comfortable in your favorite space, with your favorite drink and allow yourself to take a ride from deep inside the pine strewn wilderness to way up into the snowy northern high-lands full of lights. If you feel so inclined, let the stories reflect your own inner musings, and allow each Evergreen journey to take you with it.

My winter wish is for you to find quiet joy inside the pages of Evergreen: Tales of Winter Shadows. Settle into a gloomy day and sit with the words on these pages. It's okay to rest and grow in the shadows. As Jeanie Marshall insists in White, Green, Red "The sun must return."

Peace and Shadow,
River Eno

The End of Our Dark

Sue Westwind

When the days go to grieving
you will still see green. Flowers.
Thunderstorms. Tank tops
and short shorts. But you feel it:
we're slipping. We're all slipping.

Someone died the other day
in the extended family. Survivors
saved you no spot at the rite.
You know you are a bad fit with
the hosannas and savior theme.
They know this too. If there is
anything among human rituals
that one must not crash, it's
a funeral. Not that the dead care,
though common lore admits
their interest in the party we
pretend they miss.

We're slipping, because despite
the heat, summer is a pet that
will get itself lost for some time.

Autumn offers a way station.
Return of children to school is
the underlayment of our knowing—
oh sure, bless me with cooler breezes
and the palette of fall leaves waving,
give me festivals and fat pumpkins—
but griefs collect in the waning light
on the rush home and in the corners
of houses flickered and flooded by
hooded bulbs in every room.

We smile at little kids' costumes
for only at All Hallow's are they
tasked to say, to enact, how
the spirits step loose from the veil
that shields us. Day of the Dead.
Remembrance time, flame touched
to candle for those with courage
to set a table for the dumb supper,
where the living may not speak.

Autumn goes bleak here in November,
dressed up in one day of thanks. Long
bereft of summer's love, how we pant
for winter's flame—the solstice that
bursts the longest night into sunrise
where young men wade
into chill waters naked to the shock
of the season, emerging ravenous
for warm chocolate and wool blankets.

Onward to the work within.
Here, culture leaves you on your own.
You may discover pages that suggest
hard tasks: inner child, forgiveness,

self-loving. But what about grief?
Could it be there's more that Solstice
has to impart before the bright minutes
accumulate over months to come?

Look to the sun's vast huzzah
in snowfall—your forever furnace,
emblem of fiery grace,
driver of every season for the way
it favors—toward or away. Sun,
the wick that never burns down when
you pilgrimage in the dark or prance
to its shine. If grief were a tyrant,
the sun would not be allowed to
herald the year's shortest day.
Let the heart lead into silence as Sol
tiptoes back to your hemisphere,
flush with notes from grievers
about how every winter, every loss,
every twist in the story of Return is
gathered by all expectant sentient
hearts under the sun, blinking below
their perception or danced outright
along ley lines of tender feeling.

Cut an apple in half across its width
Sprinkle the inside with
Cinnamon, Rosemary, Mustard Seed, and
Nutmeg
Write your wish on a piece of paper and fold
it toward you
Put it in the middle of the apple and put the
halves back together
Tie them together with string
Press cloves into the apple
Put in a cool window for a week

What We Buried Here

Maddox Emory Arnold

When you open your eyes, you find yourself among the trees. The harsh winter sun sends shards of light slicing through the branches overhead, but when you look down, you see you have no shadow. This does not concern you. Why should it? You were summoned, and when one is summoned, one must answer the call.

You step soundlessly across the frozen ground as gnarled roots and detritus try to clutch at your ankles. But they cannot grasp what is not truly there, lacking any flailing limbs or battered sneakers for them to cling to. You pass through foliage where it grows too close to avoid, and it sends a jolt of *life* through you. You hardly recognize it anymore. You've been away too long.

Soon enough, you reach her. Lana, the oldest tree in this corner of the forest. Her needles are browning this deep into winter, and the dead color takes on a reddish cast in the setting sun. You stand before her, waiting. A finch alights on one of her lower branches, one of the winter birds either too stupid or too stubborn to fly south. It whispers something to the tree before flitting away.

You suddenly feel her full attention upon you. A force like that of ancient stones covered in ice that never quite melts in the summer, of roots dug in so deep they know the map to the core of the earth. The wind begins to whistle through her branches. A forest creature lumbers past, crackling debris beneath its feet. Bats swing by overhead, their wings sending velvety echoes down to reach you. In these sounds—the rhythm of the forest—the tree finds her voice.

You are late, she says.

You fight the urge to sigh. "It gets harder each time you send for me."

A boulder shifts somewhere along the nearby cliffs, indicating Lana's distaste. *He has come again. I would think you'd be eager to see him.*

You say nothing. Because yes, you should be eager. And yet, you aren't. Not anymore. "I thought you said you wouldn't call me for this again."

Lana whips her branches in sharp reprimand. *This time is different. He is not on my land.*

You pause. "Then why—"

He ventured farther this time. Away from my side of the forest. Into hers.

You're incapable of feeling cold, but the words send an impression of ice deep into your chest. You don't wait for further orders. You turn, and you run.

⚛

The first time your lover came, you found him at your grave. Or what passed for your grave, that is. Your body had never been found.

When you opened your eyes, you were deep in the forest. He was right there in front of you, close enough to touch. But when you tried, you were unable to make contact. You shouted at him. Tried to grab him, tackle him, drag him down into the grave with you.

He just kept staring at the freshly dug soil already spotted with a few stray pine needles. You didn't even know what he'd buried there. In place of a headstone,

10

you saw only a framed photograph nailed to the nearest tree. The two of you together, in your hiking gear, smiling warmly against a backdrop of spring foliage and sunbeams.

When you finally understood there was no way to make him see or hear you, you stood quietly beside him, tracing your smiles in the photograph with your eyes. You wanted to cry, but you couldn't. You wanted to dig up your own grave, but you couldn't.

You wanted him to say something, but he didn't. He left when the sun began to set.

&

You linger at the edge of Lana's territory. The woods are eerily silent, as though waiting to see what you will do. Lana requires order. That's why you like her. The forest creatures find her region peaceful. The river freezes in whirling patterns to please her. And spirits like you are allowed to rest until they are called.

But beyond the old tree's influence, there is another. Serra. She is much taller than Lana, and where the old tree likes order, this one feeds on chaos. Tremors below the earth, river rapids and mudslides.

And spirits that do not rest.

You feel them as soon as you enter Serra's realm. They call to you, their voices twining around your limbs and urging you to join in their haunting chorus of wails and whimpers. In the oncoming darkness, their shapes morph in and out of focus, like mist that can't make up its mind as to whether it wishes to coalesce or dissipate. The swirling mess of the undead roils with screaming faces before settling back into silent, groping limbs, a jumble of souls without any grip on reality.

You know you can't stay long. Lana has warned you before of the dangers of this side of the forest, the way the tortured spirits here can draw you in, make you into one of them if you get too close or listen too long.

You close your eyes and try to parse through the shrieks and moans of the spirits, the crackling branches and gusting winds. You're searching for something, searching for...*there*. Beneath the symphony of the restless forest, you hear a beating heart. The one you used to listen to each morning when you woke up. The one that won't stop beating for you, begging you to fill in the empty gaps in its rhythm.

Your eyes snap open when you realize where you must go. You begin to move again, forced to go more slowly as you try to avoid the writhing mists of livid spirits. But the urgency of that heartbeat, *his* heartbeat, calls you forward.

☯

The second time, you found him on the riverbank, a few miles from your makeshift grave. He crouched at the water's edge, staring into the patterns of ice and the rushing water beneath. He wore your coat, the one you'd always hated because it was too tight in the shoulders. You used to wear it anyway because he thought it looked good on you.

You approached warily, unsure of how this was supposed to work. After all, there was no instruction manual for how to haunt your loved ones. When you sat beside him, you saw that he was crying. If you had possessed a heart, it would have splintered in that moment. He hadn't cried at the grave, and you knew that he'd let it build in him, the way he always did. You could see it now — the pressure in his chest, the storm behind his eyes.

You did something then. You couldn't explain how, but you did it anyway. The sight of him, broken and in pain, filled you with a rage that rivaled the power of the river before you, of the cliffs beyond the forest, of the trees that held court there. You seethed at the fact that the man who had taught you what it meant to love another believed that he was alone. While you were *right there*, unable to convince him otherwise.

That anger, in all its depth and vitality, suddenly gave you a glimpse into Lana's own power, the network of life she reigned over. You were miles from her clearing, but you could see the barest thread of her strength flowing through the river, a shimmer just within reach.

So you stretched out, not with your hands but with the tendrils of the force that still held your soul together, and you *pulled*.

The river ice split with a resounding *crack*. He leaped to his feet while you rose slowly, never taking your eyes from his face. The river was angry with you, but you ignored it as you opened your mouth and called out to him.

"Ari." His name. His self. Everything you missed about him, you poured into those two syllables.

Ari whirled around, searching wildly for the source of the sound. "Who's there?" He demanded as his pain melted into panic, into an anger that almost outmatched yours. The river quickened its pace, pulling you away before you caused more damage. You felt yourself unraveling as the power you had taken washed away in the current.

"Is it you?" Ari whispered. He still couldn't see you. But he had *heard*.

You let a smile ghost across your face before the water carried you away, and you melted alongside the ice.

⁂

Ari is deep into Serra's territory, further than you've ever gone before. You do your best not to pass through the other spirits, but it's impossible to miss them all.

Each time you make contact, their voices suddenly become clear, bodiless wailing condensing into intelligible words.

Never got the chance...Still thinks I hate her...How long will he wait...I should have known they'd turn on me like that...Fresh blood, fresh blood tonight...

The onslaught of pain and vitriol threatens to overwhelm you. You quicken your pace, shaking your head to dispel the venom that tries to lodge itself there.

You find Ari stumbling over fallen branches toward the clearing where Serra resides. You try in vain to speak to him, to break through the barrier between life and death. But this side of the forest is too primal, too proud to let your voice through. Especially when the other spirits drown out your pleas with their cries.

They call to you, just as Lana warned you they would. They pull at you, pinching and poking into your ghostly form. As you draw near to Ari, the spirits seem to grow more frantic, more gleeful. They twist around you, and you can no longer avoid their shadowy mists. Their whispers fill your ears...

Yes, just leave him to us...He can't hear you, why bother?...We can take care of him, take care of you...Yes...Stay with us...

You find that these thoughts are dangerously close to your own. After all, you're dead. Why are you still looking after Ari? Lana had promised you wouldn't have to anymore, not after the last time he came. And yet, here you are, following him into danger.

The spirits seem to respond to your hesitation, writhing more quickly in the air as you hurry forward.

☖

It wasn't until Ari's fifth visit that Lana spoke to you. In the voice of river rapids and rustling branches, she informed you that it was becoming a concern, the way

Ari kept wandering through the woods, disturbing the peace. She told you it was your fault, in fact, for speaking to him that day at the riverbank.

"What?" You couldn't help feeling indignant. "It's not like I *chose* to die out here. And it's not my fault you can't control your woods."

She hadn't taken kindly to that. She'd sent you sprawling, a zap of cosmic energy that pushed you down an incline until you landed in a heap at Ari's feet.

But try as you might, you couldn't get him to listen to you again. You could no longer access Lana's power, for the forest had hidden it from you, buried deep. And Ari just kept coming, no matter the day or the time, searching for something. Searching for you. Listening for the voice you no longer knew how to use.

It took you longer than it should have to realize the woods were trying to kill him. A strategically placed branch, a rotted plank on the trail bridge, a spontaneous patch of slippery mud beside icy waters. Apparently the forest was fed up, tired of Ari's desperation ruffling the needles on too many trees' lower branches.

Luckily, by then you had learned to ride the winds and rustle certain branches of your own. Smaller actions you could manage without relying on Lana's strength. You convinced foxes to nudge the obstacles aside, sparrows to ford the bridges with hardened clay, zephyrs to cover the mud with layers of fallen foliage.

When you confronted Lana about the forest's warrant on Ari's life, she informed you in the voice of splintering ice that it was beyond her control. That the forest knew a cycle had been broken and sought to repair it however possible. The other trees had their own agency, she said, and she could not forbid them. But because she mourned any needless loss of life, she had agreed to call you back whenever Ari was in danger.

And so you returned time and time again, until it was easy to disarm the forest's weapons with a flick of the wrist, a blink or a sigh, until you were numb to the sight of your former lover, and he seemed numb to the cold.

You could stop this, you know, Lana rumbled to you once.

"I already have," you scoffed. "I save his damn life every time I'm here. Not that he ever thanks me for it."

The tree's branches rustled with what sounded suspiciously like pity. *I mean that you could stop him from coming.*

But you didn't know how. Or perhaps you did, and you simply didn't want to admit it. Perhaps you preferred to risk Ari's life, to let your love for him sour, if it meant you could see him one more time, then once more, and again the next time he came.

⚛

Serra is waiting for you. She stands at the far side of a wide clearing, cliffs arcing up and away to her left, a frozen waterfall glittering atop stone in the moonlight. Harsh shadows cling to her trunk, giving the impression of scars and craters left in her bark. She towers above all the other trees with her canopy stretched over them like a predator looming over its prey.

Ari continues forward until he stands in the center of the clearing, oblivious to the horrors that surround him.

Spirits prowl across every inch of the clearing. These are the oldest, the most solid, the worst of them. Some stand still, whimpering and gazing off into the distance while mist curls around them and punches through their chests. Others appear to be crawling across the ground, unable to stay upright. Still more swirl and flow forth with the mists. There must be hundreds of them. Here, their voices are directed not at you, but at

Serra. She drinks them in, her needles a vivid green even this deep into winter, nourished by the pain of the spirits.

You pause. If you enter the clearing, you may never leave again. This close to Serra's influence, you could find yourself trapped in her clearing forever as a broken shell of what you are. No more rest. No more peace. Haunted, inside and out.

Just like Ari. The thought comes to you unbidden, and you can't help but see the truth of it in Ari's hunched shoulders and trembling hands.

Suddenly, the spirits' voices fall away. The mists freeze in place, some spirits left half-formed and others frozen in silent, agonized screams. Ari, too, seems unable—or unwilling—to move.

So. She knows you are here.

Ahh, she whispers, her voice the deadly impact of icicles against frozen ground. *It's been so long since we last spoke, Rule-Breaker.*

☙

You'd met Serra only once before. The forest had laid a trap, a clever one for once. Ari was meant to travel along the cliffs, to where rockslides were common and came on suddenly—a constant threat to hikers with inadequate gear or subpar footwear. You knew the danger all too well.

Furious, you sent the boulder meant for Ari's head crashing down too soon, early enough to scare him off and send him back toward home. You let him go. The forest wouldn't try to take his life again. Not today, at least.

But your rage remained strong, pulsing from within your empty chest. Serra must have heard it radiating out from so high on the cliffs. And so she sent a messenger.

A raven alighted on the boulder that was meant to kill Ari. Its eyes bored into yours as it cocked its head, dropped a small bundle to the ground, and flew off once more. Curiosity pushed your anger aside for the moment, and you approached the bundle.

It was a small bunch of pine needles, tied together with a thin, supple twig. You knelt before it, then passed your fingers through the needles.

Her voice arrived swiftly, sharp and brittle in tones of cracking ice and a hunter's bowstring. *I've heard stories of you,* Serra whispered in your ear, projecting the words through what must have been needles from her uppermost branches. *The spirit who defies the natural order of things. But why…*

Her voice was like a dagger, cutting deep, but soon enough it began to drip with aging sap and ridicule. *All this, for one man? I am disappointed. My spirits watch him, but his desperation is worthless to me.*

"Don't talk about him that way," you hissed. Your hand was frozen in place; it looked like the needles were piercing through your skin.

Interesting. The sap in her voice crystallized and formed jagged corners once more. *Your passion would do you credit in my woods. Consider this a formal invitation. That is, if you can stand to leave him behind…*

You squeezed your eyes shut as you tried to pry yourself from her grasp.

So angry, she mused. Her presence suddenly pressed in on you like a vice, the edges of her voice slicing into your very core. *Come to me when you're ready, Rule-Breaker.*

And then she was gone. A sudden wind tossed the bundle of needles off the edge of the cliff. It left you feeling empty, your rage burned up in a single flare of defiance.

You stood watching the moon rise until you felt the familiar pull of Lana's influence once more. You went willingly, seeking sleep's oblivion. This time, though, you slept fitfully.

◬

I wondered when you'd come to visit me. Serra's voice rips through you like shattered glass. *And you've brought an offering, I see.* The spirits nearest Ari slowly begin to move again, curling around him. Ari gasps, freed from his momentary paralysis. The despair is so strong here that even he must be able to feel it.

"Leave him alone." You try to keep the tremor out of your voice. "I came to bring him back."

That's rich, the tree snarls. *Seeing as you're the reason he's here in the first place.*

She whips out her branches with an echoing *crack,* and the spirits near you resume their slow dance as well. They cackle as their faces melt in and out of view. You open your mouth to refute the tree's claim, but you can't. Because you know she's right.

I know you called to him, once, she rumbles. *That's why he still comes to the trees. He knows you're here. And you, little Rule-Breaker, simply cannot let go.*

The mist begins to condense around you, and you see it wrap around Ari, too, at the center of the clearing. The spirits gleefully add their voices to the tree's barbs. *Your fault...Too selfish to say goodbye...Look at what you've done...*

Ari cries out and puts his hands over his ears, falling to his knees. You stand frozen, forced to watch his pain made manifest.

The tree makes a sympathetic sound in a burst of gelid wind. *You could simply let us have him, leave him to us. Think of it. You'd finally be free...*

You hesitate. And you hate yourself for it. Because deep down, you know the pain Ari is feeling. It's reflected in your own pitiful, ghostly half-life. You, however, have the advantage of blissful inexistence whenever Ari is away. He has to live with your absence each day, paired cruelly with the instinct that you're still there somehow, just out of reach. And you know, too, that you are responsible for that instinct. The day you said his name, you set him on this path.

You squeeze your eyes shut. You could end it. No more saving Ari's life, no more watching him break down. A part of you is tempted to take the easy way out. But the larger part, the one you've tried to bury, the one that still loves him—that part of you screams louder.

"No," you whisper, voice barely audible above the spirits' grotesque laughter. "I won't let you take him."

Serra sighs, the wind in her voice expanding into a hailstorm. *Suit yourself, Rule-Breaker.*

The spirits around you suddenly draw back, and you feel a shift in the air. Ari lets out a strangled gasp. You open your eyes.

He's looking right at you. It almost feels like you have a heart again, the way your chest hitches. He can *see* you.

"Ari," you breathe.

"It's you." He starts to reach for you.

And the spirits descend upon you again.

They smother Ari first, wrestling him to the ground. Ari screams, and you try to move toward him, but the spirits leap upon you as well. Serra pours her power into them, allowing them to tear into you. They rip back the layers of your essence as your scream joins their wailing cacophony. They begin to unravel the threads that tether you to the waking world, ravaging the part of you that still longs to hear Ari's voice one last time.

♢

The last time Ari came had been difficult. The forest didn't even try to kill him—he seemed ready to do it himself. You watched him, as you always did, and tried to find within yourself the love you once had for him. It was harder than it should have been, smaller now, a fraction of what it once was. You watched Ari stumble across the path, his nose and eyes red with cold, with grief. You followed him up to the cliffs, to where Serra had first spoken to you.

You did nothing as he stopped at the edge of the path. You did nothing as the tears froze on his cheeks. You did nothing as he stared down a sheer rock face to the ground far below. As he heaved a broken sob from an empty chest. As he closed his eyes. You did nothing.

But you were never good at leaving things alone.

Before he could take the next step, you gestured for a nearby snowy owl to show herself. She complied, for she had never liked how the forest treated Ari, and she swooped down to land on a nearby rock shelf. Ari faltered. She cooed sorrowfully at him.

Then, Ari looked at you. There was no way he could have seen you, but you stood frozen, pinned beneath his gaze. The owl cooed once more. Ari shifted to stare back at the abyss splayed out beneath him. A thin, ugly smile drifted across his lips before he abruptly turned, and left.

The owl blinked at you and flew off, but you stayed to watch Ari go. When he disappeared from sight, swallowed once more by the spiteful trees of the forest, Lana spoke to you. She took pity on you, said she would continue the work of keeping Ari alive without dragging you back again. To spare you from having to see him.

Then you, too, were gone.

⚐

You feel yourself fading, melting into the mist that flows in and around your body. Serra revels in your undoing, feeds on your screams, and you feel her power twisting your soul, preparing to rip it away.

But you hear Ari screaming, too. Over the mass of spirits shrieking their delight, Ari's voice pierces through all other sound, all other fear. And the sound of his pain is worse than anything Serra or the spirits could do to you.

Flailing for some way to save him, you find that you recognize something in the tree's power. All the despair vibrating through the clearing—it fills you with the same energy you had used to speak to Ari, so long ago. Serra's network of power, fervent and vast in its proximity to the tree herself, a twisted snarl of pain and darkness that radiates out through her entire domain. You see all of it, splayed like a spider's web. And you know what you have to do.

You reach out as you did once before, grabbing hold of Serra's power and *yanking* against it. The spirits suddenly retreat, just far enough to create a path from you to Ari. The mists form a tunnel around you, faces and limbs appearing to press against the invisible barrier. Your entire being thrums with the power, so much more than you had held before, but you push it aside to stare at Ari. To see him finally seeing you.

Ari approaches slowly. You drink each other in, eyes roving across every inch of one another's bodies. Then, Ari smiles, and it is the single most beautiful thing you have ever seen.

"Ari—" you start, but he cuts in.

"I knew you were here. I knew you were waiting for me." He reaches for you, overjoyed. But his fingers pass right through your palms.

"No, my love." The words warp across your tongue, after so long unspoken. *My love.* "I'm not really here. Not the way you are."

His smile fades slightly. He tries again, raising a hand to your cheek, but you are still inaccessible to him. "But...you spoke to me."

"Yes. I'm sorry. I didn't mean to keep you here. I just—" Your voice breaks, and you feel something that should have been impossible: tears sliding down your cheeks. "I was too afraid of being alone."

And there it is. The truth you've buried, the shame you've kept secret by reflecting it outward upon anyone and anything else but yourself. Your fear. Your heart, no longer in your chest. Ari is crying too, now, but the growing wail of the spirits above reminds you that you don't have much time.

"You have to go, Ari," you tell him, voice thick with tears. "And I have to let it happen this time."

"But—"

"Please, Ari. I love you. But we have to end this."

Ari studies you for a moment, regret and longing painted across his face. But then he nods. "I love you, too." And that's all you need. You know he won't return. You know he will heal. He will live on.

"Tell me one thing," you say, suddenly desperate.

"Anything."

"What did you bury at the grave?"

Ari smiles again, dimmer this time, but still magnificent. "Your old hiking shoes," he says. "The ones you couldn't bring yourself to throw away, even though they were practically falling apart."

You laugh, but a violent push against your chest cuts it short. Serra is growing impatient. It's time for Ari to go while he still can. He reaches for you again, concerned, but you step back. Turning away, you hold out a hand toward the path to Lana's territory. You use your remaining strength to expand the tunnel in the mists and create a route for Ari back to safety.

You turn back to him and try to smile. "Time to go, love."

"You're not coming?" He asks, voice small.

You shake your head. "Not this time. Be safe."

Ari holds your gaze a moment more before he heads up the path and disappears one final time.

You hold the tunnel in place as long as you can against the onslaught from Serra and her spirits. Her power slams up against the barrier as she rages, howling in the gale that rips through her branches. You know there is no coming back from this. You would not have been able to return with Ari, not while maintaining the path. Not without Serra's strength so close, the incensed passion of the spirits in the clearing.

As soon as Ari crosses into Lana's territory, you feel the power begin to wane. The tunnel shrinks, the spirits grow louder, and soon enough, you're lying flat on your back, staring up at the trees outlined in the moonlight. The spirits shriek as they descend upon you. Serra reclaims her power and raises it high to land the final blow.

But just before she begins to swing, you feel something. A tiny trickle of energy sneaking through the collapsing tunnel in the mists. You recognize it immediately. A gift from the oldest tree. You reach for it, just managing to catch it before Serra can make you into one of her own. The familiar pull grips you, and you fade from the clearing just as the spirits converge on the place where you had been.

You sleep, finally. And you dream of him.

Return to Sender
If someone is doing you wrong
Write their name on a piece of paper
Fold the paper away from you
Put it under the sole of your shoe
Wear the shoes and walk
Walk on them like they walked on you
The harder and longer, the more you give back to
them what they gave you

The Unwatched Hour

Jordan King-Lacroix

Hy stood in the doorway, watching as Rosie Morgenstern approached. He would love to see her smile again, as he had — only once — at a Rosh Hashanah dinner. Most of the time, though, she looked down at her shoes, at the dirt of the road, or up at the sky. She had once said something about wanting to be a leaf on the wind, to blow around without a care, but he couldn't remember it now.

"Mama just wanted me to let you know that we were still coming," Rosie said. "She's fixing her kugel for tonight."

"Great to hear," Hy said. "Your mama makes great kugel."

Rosie nodded. A short silence fell between them. Hy wanted to speak, but found that some part of him didn't want to disturb her. Rosie just looked at the mezuzah on the doorjamb. She was staring at it as if it were the books she always had her nose buried in. Just as Hy was about to speak, she nodded again.

"Okay," she said. "I'll see you tonight."

And with those last words, she turned and walked off. Hy internally berated himself for not speaking. As time went on, he found that he enjoyed the company of Rosie Morgenstern more and more, and he was hoping that he might be deemed a suitable match for her. His own mother, he knew, had been busybodying about it to whoever would listen. He hoped this didn't turn Rosie sour on him.

"It's *Tekufat Tevet* tonight," Hy's mother said as Hy closed the door. She was cleaning the house, trying to make it neat for dinner with the family. "Pour out any water we have stored. Anything, all of it."

"Mum, that's a waste," Hy said, helping his mother clean.

"A waste, he says, a waste. If you can find enough iron vessels to store it all in, or iron nails to dip into them, then be my guest."

The people of their town — a small *shtetl* that wasn't on any map — were very superstitious about the turning of the *tekufot*, the cycle of the seasons. Each equinox and solstice had its own rituals and fears. Water left standing or stored in the first hour of any of these would make the body bloated and sick, even cause someone to die. Hy's mother had always told him it was because, during the first hour of every *tekufah*, the angels were changing guard. This meant that no one was watching out for the malevolent spirits who liked to swim in stored and standing water. Chava's mum said it was because, on *Tekufat Nisan*, that all the waters of Egypt turned red with blood, but Hy's mum dismissed that with a spit.

"What does she know?" his mother said. "She never read Talmud in her life, only repeats what her *mumzer* brother says."

"Do we even have to do this?" Hy asked. "It's probably fine."

His mother whirled on him, her eyes wild. "Fine, he says? Fine?"

Hy backed up, bumping into the dining table. His mother advanced on him, poking one bony finger into his chest. The fear in her eyes made his stomach drop.

"Not fine," she said. "Not fine. We are unguarded in that hour. You know that *shedim* and *dybbukim* come out to play when the night is long. They search, they swim, they frolic. And you would drink their bathwater? Bring their evil, their stink, into your body?"

"No, of course not."

"Do you want to ingest the dirt from the talons of a sheyd's cock's feet? Or the rot of a dybbuk's filth?"

"No, mama, I—" Hy started, but his mother wasn't done.

"You remember your uncle Chaim?" his mother said, spitting on the ground. "Do you?"

"Of course, mama."

His mother began to weep, collapsing in a heap at the table. Hy knew that, in times like these, all he could do was comfort her.

"I miss him," she said, through her tears. "Every day. But he strayed from the wisdom, and now his mind is gone."

"Yes, mama."

"You'll never do the same, will you, Hy? My little Hymie?" She grabbed his face, her eyes burning. Her stare penetrated through him.

"No, mama," Hy said. "Never."

As if by magic, she sobered and stood.

"Good boy," she said. "Now, finish up here. I have to go pick up something last-minute from Mandelbaum's store."

And with that, she was gone.

Hy loved his mother, but she could be a handful. Especially since his father had absconded, stating one day that he had been "called to study" and left no indication of wherever it was that he was going. That last memory of him, turning out the door with his flat cap on, made Hy spit.

"May all his teeth fall out," Hy whispered in Yiddish. "Except for one. And in that one, may he have such a toothache."

Hy set about gathering all the vessels of water they had in the house. He collected them all on the dining table. They sat before him, accusatory. Iron nails or iron vessels. Surely, he thought, they must have some around. Wasting all of this water seemed more of a sin than keeping it.

He went out to the back shed, where his family kept all the *tchotchkes* that collected over a lifetime. His father and him had built the shed together when he was younger. The memory was happy, if tainted. The shed stood strong in the backyard, such as it was. Chickens ran about mindlessly.

Inside, the shed was dark. There was a small gas lamp next to the entryway that he lit, but he knew that if he kept it on too long—and wasted too much fuel— his mother would be angry with him. He figured he had a little bit of time because whenever his mother went to Mandelbaum's store, she remained behind to chat with the owner and his wife, local gossip and news that had arrived by word of mouth. It was a twenty-minute walk there and back, so he gave himself a full hour to seek out the necessary items.

Jars of bric-a-brac filled the shelves, as well as garden implements and home repair tools. Hy felt he knew about as much about fixing cabinetry as Yitzchak the carpenter, and as much about gardening as any of the farmers in town. When you had no money, there was no option but to fix it yourself. Hy's mother did so much, it was the least he could do to keep the home in good working order if he could.

On one shelf he found a tool box filled with assorted screws and nails. Next to this, there were two small iron jugs with screw-top lids. These were prized possessions, and his mother had never figured out what to put inside them. Well, tonight would be their debut.

Hy brought his prizes inside and set to work. The two metal jugs he filled with water and screwed the caps on, placing them back in the pantry. For the rest, he began sorting through the screws and nails. He knew that if he used anything that wasn't pure iron, his mother would make him remove it and throw out the water anyway. No point taking any chances there.

Sorting through the loose items, he counted out seven nails that he was positive were pure iron. The others looked to be steel, and some too rusted to be of any use, as they would surely ruin the water with their impurities.

He dropped the nails into the vessels of water. When he'd dropped the last one, he realized he was one short. The final container was a small bottle, something he often used to carry water when he was out in the garden. Seeing as he had no belief in this superstition anyway, he pocketed the bottle. What his mother didn't know wouldn't hurt her.

As he finished his task, his mother returned home. Hy rushed to help her with her last-minute purchases, which appeared to be the majority of the meal she was preparing that night.

"Did you clear out the water?" she asked, setting right away to chopping and dicing.

"No need, mama," Hy said. "I found enough nails for them all, and I used our two iron jugs with the screw tops."

"The iron jugs?" she said, looking stricken. "But they're for a special occasion!"

"What better occasion to use them than this, mama?" Hy said. "Saving water on the night of *tekufah*?"

"And the nails, were they all iron?" she asked, eyeing him. "Only iron, none of this steel. They *shedim* are not tricked by steel."

"Pure iron, mama," Hy said, smiling. He set to helping his mother with the cooking. "I promise. This year, we waste no water."

She smiled at her son. "You're a good boy, Hymie. Always trying to help me look after this family."

In amicable silence the two set about cooking the meal. Due to the heat of the stove, Hy often found his throat getting a little tickle, which he doused with a sip of water from the flask he hid in his pocket. Each sip, it seemed, just made him thirstier.

⚚

That night, as the sun set, everyone was seated and the food had been served. Mr Mandelbaum led the prayers, for he and his wife usually joined Hy's family on special occasions since their children had died at the hands of the Cossacks. Those brutes had also taken the patriarch of the Morgenstern family, the widow and daughter of whom joined them this evening.

"*Ameyn*," the group chanted together, before commencing their meal.

Hy cleared his throat, repeating the sound several times.

"You're not getting sick, are you?" his mother asked, leaning over to touch his forehead.

"Mama, stop," Hy said. "I'm fine. Just a tickle in my throat. It must have been the dust in the shed."

"What were you looking for in the shed?" Rosie asked.

"Iron nails," Hy said. He tried to act aloof, but he was bad at it.

"What for?" she asked. The faintest hint of a smile etched her face. Hy's heart fluttered at the sight of it.

"To prove to me that he is smarter than I am," Hy's mother said, laughing.

"Mama said that, in order to not have to throw away the water on *Tekufat Tevet*, we would need iron nails to place in the containers of water, or iron vessels to hold it," Hy said. "So, I went looking — and found — the necessary nails."

"And used my good screw-top containers, too," his mother said, scoffing, but smiling also.

"To not waste water is a *mitzvah*," Mr Mandelbaum said. "That was good thinking, my boy."

Hy smiled with pride.

"He gets the good brains from my side," his mother said. "Can't have been from my *shmendrik* of a husband, who won't even give me a *get*!"

It was true, and was quite the scandal. Hy's father would not consent to give his wife a *get* of divorce before leaving. And since no one knew where to find him, his mother would likely remain an *agunah*, a chained woman, until she died. It was one of the things that bothered Hy the most about his father's leaving. Leave if you want, he thought, but at least free the family from you in full.

"We'll find him," Mrs Mandelbaum said. "If anyone can do it, it's those Rapaport boys. They know how to track down men like your husband."

"From your mouth to God's ears," his mother said, knocking on the wooden table.

The tickle in Hy's throat became too much to bear and he secreted a sip — the last of the water — from his little flask. At last, the little tickle ceased. He must have washed the last of that damnable dust away.

Something caught Hy's eye, then. A strange, dark mote of dust floated by. Looking at it seemed to hurt his eyes, as if a sharp pin were being pushed into his pupil.

Looking around the table, he noticed that something was wrong with everyone's faces. They were all looking at him, even though their eyes were also looking at each other. Their mouths were moving in conversation, but he couldn't understand a word. To his horror, Hy watched as the skin began to melt from the faces of the collected guests.

He stood, knocking his chair over. Everyone's head swivelled to look at him. His breath caught in his throat, and his vision blanked.

"Hymie," his mother asked. "What's wrong?"

Hy stood there, his body stiff, his jaw grinding his teeth back and forth.

"Is he having a seizure?" Rosie asked.

In a voice that was both Hy's and not Hy's, a string of nonsense words issued from his mouth.

"*Got in himl,*" Mr Mandelbaum said.

Hy turned his eyes upon the man, looking from him to his wife. Then, in a new voice, spoke.

"Your children suffer without their parents," the voice said. "We made sure it was so. You abandoned them, and so we took them, brought the Cossacks upon them."

The Mandelbaum's gasped.

"Hymie, what are you saying?" his mother asked. Tears welled in her eyes. She went to grab at Hy's shirt, but he shirked her.

"Lousy husband leaves a chained woman with a brat who won't listen," Hy said, turning on his mother. "A *shnook* who doesn't believe. You have failed as a wife, as a mother, and as a woman. You will die alone."

Hy's mother cried out. She pulled at her hair, overcome with grief. Mrs Mandelbaum went to her, cried with her.

As Hy turned on the Morgensterns, there was the sound of glass shattering. Rosie looked at the ground and saw the small glass flask that Hy had been drinking from.

"Hy didn't find a nail for all the vessels, did he?" Rosie asked.

Hy laughed. "No. All it took was a small nudge to get him to drink at the right time."

"A *sheyd*!" Hy's mother cried. "A *sheyd* has my boy!"

The *sheyd* who had control of Hy laughed. His voice was hoarse and unpleasant.

"I can see across the worlds," the *sheyd* said. "I can tell you where to find your lost husband."

"I make no deals with filth," Hy's mother said.

"My deal would be to make him give you your rightful *get*," the *sheyd* said. "All you would need to do is allow me to keep this body."

"What?" she said. "No."

"It would only be for a time," the *sheyd* said. "I have many things to do."

"A *get*," she said, her voice sounding far away. "At last, I would be free."

"No, Tzippy," Mrs Mandelbaum said. "No, you cannot bargain away your boy's soul."

"I can summon your children's souls," the *sheyd* said to Mrs Mandelbam. "Let you speak with them one last time, ensure their place in the world after."

"Deceiver," Mr Mandelbaum said. "We cannot trust a single thing you say, get out!"

The *sheyd* gestured at Mr Mandelbaum, and he fell to the floor, clutching at his chest. Mrs Morgenstern ran to his aid, offering him water.

"Without a doctor, he'll die," the *sheyd* said. "I can make sure one is summoned."

"We will make no deals," Rosie said. Her quiet voice was stern.

The *sheyd* turned to face her.

"There is always a deal to be struck," the *sheyd* said. "What do you want?"

"Nothing," Rosie said. "I desire nothing."

"Lies," the *sheyd* said. "Not a single human, since the dawn of Creation, has ever desired nothing."

"Then I am she," Rosie said, smirking. "Unique among all the people of the world."

"I could kill you," the *sheyd* said. "What care I if you do not agree to any terms?"

"I've read about your kind," Rosie said. "From your behaviour tonight, it seems like you are a corrupted helper *sheyd*. You have done nothing but try to strike deals since you arrived."

"You know nothing of me," the *sheyd* said. "Do not try and know that which is unknowable to you."

Rosie laughed. "You are not unknowable. Your kind has been known by ours since you first appeared. Take this deal, I can give you this. Feh, I say. You desperately desire a body. Why? What happened to your own? Where are your cock's feet?"

The *sheyd* hissed at her, drawing Hy's mouth wide. His eyes bulged, and his teeth gave the appearance of being long and pointed.

"You might as well tell me, *sheyd*," Rosie said. "Seeing as it's obvious that you cannot leave here with Hy's body until you have bargained for it."

The *sheyd* cast his sinister glance at the collected people. Mr Mandelbaum lay still on the cold ground, Mrs Morgenstern doing her best to help him.

"My body was destroyed," the *sheyd* said. "I was in a great battle. I helped your kind, and you destroyed me. But my spirit, my essence, I cast out into the ether of the world and here, now, do I land; inside the body of a boy on the night of *Tekufah Tevet*. It has been a long, long wait. And I desire vengeance."

"Vengeance," Rosie said. "Is that all?"

"It is everything!" the *sheyd* bellowed.

Rosie contemplated this. She looked at everyone collected there that night. At Tzippy and Hy, chained to their absent patriarch. At the Mandelbaums, shadows of themselves since the death of their children. And finally, at her mother, lost since her own husband was buried.

For as long as Rosie could remember, even before her father's death, she had desired nothing more than to feel nothing at all. Each day, each moment of existence was pain for her. It was not a physical pain; it was a yearning within her soul. Nothing made her happy. The only thing she thought of each night as she went to sleep, and as she awoke each morning, was the bliss of nothingness. Unlike her parents, she did not have faith in the Lord, their supposed creator. Even now, confronted with the supernatural, that only proved these beings existed, not that God did. No, Rosie had wanted nothing more in her whole life than to die. And, finally, she felt she had found a time to do so with purpose.

"Take my life," Rosie said. "Take my life, have your vengeance on mankind, and then release Hy and begone from our world forever."

"No, no, no," Mrs Morgenstern cried. "No, Rosie, please. What are you doing?"

"Fulfilling my life's desire," she said. "At this, the unwatched hour, when no angel can intervene to save me."

"No, please, I—"

"Deal," the *sheyd* said.

"One last condition," Rosie said.

The *sheyd* growled. "Name it."

Hy looked down at everyone. Why was he standing? Why were his mother and Mrs Mandelbaum crying? Why were Mr Mandelbaum and Mrs Morgenstern on the floor?

"What's going on?" Hy asked, sitting down. His chair leg crunched on some glass, but he didn't know what had broken.

"I," his mother said. "I don't know. There was a great sadness, I think."

"Yes," Mrs Mandelbaum said. "There was."

"But I don't remember what it was," Tzippy said.

"Neither do I," Mrs Morgenstern said.

"And now it's gone."

"Yes, gone."

"Can someone help me up?" Mr Mandelbaum said. Hy leaned down, helping to pull the man into his chair once more.

Mrs Morgenstern looked around, uncertain and unspeaking, before taking her place at the table again. Silence fell on all the guests. Although no one had any memory of what had happened, they all felt—a sensation they couldn't vocalize, could not convey to the others there—a great weight in their chests. Hy felt a hole in his mind, the shape and size of, he didn't know who. A girl, he thought. Someone he knew? If so, it must have been long ago, for he only remembered a whisper of her now. And even that was fading quickly.

"Shall we eat?" Tzippy said. "The food is getting cold."

And so, they ate. And somewhere, in the world between worlds, a young girl who desired nothing more than nothingness smiled.

White, Green, Red

Jeannie Marschall

The sun must return
no matter the shadows
no matter the cold
the sun must return

We fight through the snowbanks
to where ancients grow
to waken the red dawn
the sun must return

Sensing the creatures that watch from the trunks as
our chants push the stillness away, lah, away
our freshly cut offerings placed green on white because
now, here, and always
the sun must return

But no light shows the colours unless we are willing
no warmth without warmth spilling forth, then we see
on the white, in the green, living red in the light, holy,
only in giving
the sun will return

Florida Water

   for Cleansing
your Home

Put in a jar:
Lemongrass
Sage
Dried orange peels
Cinnamon Sticks
Bay leaves
Dried Roses
Clear Quartz
Lavender
Rosemary

Fill Jar with Vodka and Moon water
And let steep for one month
Strain and put in a diffuser to spray
around corners, doorways, and in places
where the energy is dark or stale

The Whispers of Woods

C.L. Roldan

The darkness; it's where my mother is. She lives deep in the woodland crevice, as it holds her tightly in its dirt hand. The family doesn't speak of her nor her foolish escape for something other than chores and children bearing and rearing. She ran across the mist field behind the estate of our home.

Leaving us behind in her search for something better than the mundane of family. Or that is what my father described it as.

"*How selfish,*" he whined over dark liquor. Remaining ever so bothered that one might want to leave him, his debt, arrogance and sloth.

"*How sad,*" the maids cried feverishly as they washed her old clothes.

My mother was beloved but I do not remember her ever being well liked. Everyone loved the way she smiled or baked a sweet confection. They thought how she tied my sister's and I's hair with ribbons was endearing. But they didn't like her worrying thoughts, or her opinion on important matters. Even the cooks and maids thought her eventually too demanding when requested a quick change in decoration or meal. They loved a memory of her but never her.

I'm wearing a dollish old dress she could no longer wear after she had my eldest sister. The button is coming undone as am I.

The maids flock around like service bound hens, laying garlands of ivy and holly for solstice tonight. Symbols of fertility in the old world where this tradition was celebrated. Though my father wants no more of us as we only bring him great pain. I only find it to be a fitting exchange he is none the wiser to.

The winter solstice is not something many acknowledge in this time in the brushes and cliff edged Northern Ireland. I find myself having a certain kinship with it. Lost things are always found. It must be embedded in us, branded in our blood somehow — these old stories we worship. On this day the sun had set at his earliest reprieve and an ice slicked night would cast itself over us all. I remembered my nanny, the one who lives in our downstairs quarters now, used to read to me the solstice tales her mother read to her. I'd laugh at the Holly King's arrogance. *How can anyone think they'd rule forever?* I'd giggle.

She'd look down at me and hum, "Those who gain their power from misery think they can do whatever they want and drag us all down with them."

I nodded carrying her wisdom like a locket.

Outside had been ice bitten, and the sun had already set hours before. Only the darkness was at our fingertips now, and I could feel my soul stir in its presence. Small crowds gathered below my frosted window, and a bonfire sat at the center of the backyard.

I could see my sisters were prancing around with fistfuls of mistletoe, running to handsome boys in their dull suits, stealing kisses on the cheek. My youngest brother was fussing around in our nanny's arms and was swatting at invisible flies, crying that something was biting him. Our nanny shushed him and said to settle himself or else he'd be put to bed before the festivities even began.

I felt poorly for the boy as I knew what was nipping at his soft skin. I looked down at the book mesmerized by its coloring and scripture. I've held it close since my mother's disappearance, and it's led me to a certain hope. I can find her, I know where she is and who must have her. She left this book for me and I alone. The same stories she only read to me when I was just a girl.

I hugged the old yellowing pages to my chest in a great embrace as my father barreled through my door. The mahogany creaked, but it didn't startle me like it would the young woman I was only a year ago.

He was wearing his navy button shirt and black slacks, his hair slicked with something gelled, and he smelled like scotch and cigars. A cold wind smacked my face as it followed behind him, biting the tip of my nose.

"Why haven't you made your way downstairs?"

I remained staring at the floor. People had been saying I've been strange since my mother left. I wasn't strange, just patient. But I must admit to my faults, it feels easier to do this knowing where my fate lies now. What will become of me by the end of night...I almost let myself grin if it had not felt too intense. I didn't want to give my family hope. I didn't enjoy much lately; it was like my spirit dislocated itself from my soul. Those who think they are the same are foolish. One is the base of existence and the other is the one that sparks interest in it.

My sisters stopped asking me to attend the market with them, and my tutor hadn't been able to make out my strange handwriting in months. He didn't understand that I had to practice. The lucid lettering of the spirited people was far more important than the teachings of current affairs. They would whisper, my family, asking themselves why I had let my hair turn to mats, why my skin grew bumped and red. Why they never saw my plain white teeth anymore. I could scarcely smile, scarcely breathe. It was and has been an endless night.

"We have to pull the day back to us, come." My father offered his hand, but I only clutched the book harder. He sighed and his footsteps creaked the floor's tender spots as he came towards me.

"There's no real reason for you to be here Bridgette. Celebrate with the rest of us, with the ones who didn't leave."

When I followed him back downstairs I almost hugged him, I almost told him how sorry I was. But the hallway remained quiet, I bit my tongue and swallowed my sorrows as I couldn't betray myself. Stick candles placed delicately lit the dim house, and the yule log burned in its hearth, pouring its warm spice into every room.

Outdoors, everyone was smiling, toasting in good health to one another awaiting for the end of a long night.

They think she was a child for what she did, running into an uncertain woods but if they knew what beheld it at night, on this night, they might have understood. My mother grasped a great truth, as do I. We are not crafted, not made for something this plain, or this brutal. To live is to suffer with an audience. Instead of taking a bow she bolted off the stage.

In the morning light, when the night no longer held its dominance, they couldn't find her. Only I knew why, and I alone.

I stood in the middle of the yard watching as children and dogs chased each other and couples held their new babes. The massive bonfire ripped its flames back and forth as if taunting me. And I stared far too long for it to be considered proper. But nobody was paying mind to what I did or did not do. They enjoyed the festivities amongst themselves, peering at the stars above in absolute wonderment they couldn't contain.

The grandmothers gathered the children on the other side of the bonfire and began weaving the tale of solstice. How the Oak King would triumph tonight if they all obeyed. He'd slay the Holly bastard, one said.

"I'll help him!" A boy in a suit he was growing too tall for declared.

The old woman laughed. "That is not for us to interfere with boy, we only aid our day king with these fires, may he follow its smoke through the trees," she said.

My sister offered me a glass of something warm and tried to comment on my dress, even in its ruining condition. I nodded and drank, and she eventually joined the others. I could feel my father approach me and stood behind as we both let the fire warm our dull skin and cold bones.

"She was very troubled, dear."

I only looked ahead. Past the fire lay the woods. It was almost time. I knew what he was going to say.

He grabbed my hand urgently. "You couldn't have begged her to stay. She stopped listening a long time ago."

I let my hand fall from his. "You did first."

"Sometimes I just don't understand you; I'm afraid there's nothing here for you." He sighed.

"I fear that too," I said quietly. I wasn't sure if he heard it. If he had, the cooks were too loud causing a crack in our conversation when they announced the main course's entrance. The flayed pig carried out glossed in gold crust and roasted potato arranged around it like a small garden.

The hour was upon us it seemed. The flame grew higher in front of me as it did for my mother last year. I always promised myself I'd trace the ghost of her footsteps, follow the trail of peony and rose.

As the bright orange streaks almost licked the sky everyone cheered and began to eat. I stepped back and away. From here, at the beginning of the woods, a coldness drew to the back of me. Whispering sweet nothings into my neck, almost tracing its swiftness into my hand as if to grab it. As if to say, *it's time.*

It's true, what they say about the savagery of winter and its kin, the night. Cold nights make us far bolder than what we can deliver. It rings us dry of our senses, and we step fiercely onto the slick grounds salivating to have us slip. But I was fine with foolishness, it was a relief of the dread that cradled my face in a judgmental manner.

It was an inherited otherness I realized, that made each step backward easier. I stood a long distance away from the party and my house. The trail into the forest began just one more step back.

I recited the words I knew they'd hear. The strange foreign tongue I practiced from that old book. The whispers started behind me in response. The small gold traced the air like a glowing fabric. One might mistaken it for a spark of fire, but I knew they were here before they showed themselves. I could feel it, deep in my curdling blood. And their voices were a soft melody that I wished was louder. All I had to do was follow. The pine needles pricked the palms of my hand as I took each step backward. I let the cold grip of the forest take hold of my hand as it led me to its wide-open mouth. How strange, how easy it was to slip away, and rush into a near pitch dark background of green hedges and thick tall trees. The voices were pleading, some giggling as if it were all a joke. Others were more demanding. But all of which I could hear, and all I paid my attention to.

I strolled breathlessly into the start of the woods, where it lay open ahead. In the winter-touched shrubbery, snow collected on the naked branches, and the gold specs grew brighter against its whiteness. The gold darts kept singing a song, in what I imagine was the strange cursive I'd been seeing in my dreams, the one I had been writing down constantly in my notebooks. They led me through the strangely thick brackens, and I shivered when they took me all the way to the heart of the woods.

In the clearing this place was like no other. A labyrinth of green amongst a dim forest where the trees were sharper, and the ground began to hum with something ancient. The trees moved ever so slightly as if they were breathing, and the roots and dead leaves scattered the ground lit by something unnatural to the natural world. A greenish hue kindled beneath me like a string of veins etching the ground, pumping the green and blue blood of the earth in its rapid pulse.

In this new light I could see the translucent wings carrying the coin sized bodies of fairies. The way they chased each other in quick succession, and I felt their nipping at my fingertips as I reached out to them in the open air.

An owl cooed and a soft patter of water falling into a body of a small pond somewhere gentled my heart's racing beats ever so slightly. It was no wonder my mother had found her place here. It was no wonder that she wanted to stay. I smiled, for the first time, I let my face know joy. I bared my teeth in pleasure of the world and laughed at the wood's grandeur.

"Mother!" I shouted. My voice joined the chorus of the earth's hum and was merely drowned out by it. I shouted again and again. I walked further and further feeling excitement tickle my feet and throat. The golden fairies raced around me, singing their song, but as I kept going it began to sound sad.

"Mother!" I shouted, this time in anger.

I tripped, as though a root came from the ground and grabbed hold of my ankle. I hit my head and for a moment, I could only hear the foreboding whispers and tunes from the fairies. I pulled myself up and felt my skin had already begun bruising. I fell onto something hard, tall and scattered beneath me. It was pearl white amongst the glowing ground, and my voice snagged inside myself when I realized I fell onto a collection of bones.

I couldn't smell the peony anymore, just the salted pine, and the ghoulish song of the fairies sounded more like a taunt than a tune. Their voices were hushed but vicious. "Mother! Mother!" They imitated my howls, my cries.

I became ill quickly. I couldn't move. My mind left me immediately.

The bones were withered and loose on the floor, making up the Arrangement that was once a person. I pushed them away from me in a panic and began to sob. My hands were scraped and my voice was hoarse. The places where my skin met the remains burned at the contact and I struggled to sit up again. When I did the bones completely vanished in front of my eyes.

This place was a constant trick and my head swelled within its uncertainty.

"Have you come to take them?"

I followed a calm voice to find a tall man in white and green layered garbs. They were smeared red and black, and by the way he stood, I thought it was his blood.

"What?" I said in a small voice.

"Oh dear, they're gone now. Apologies I cannot see quite well enough in this dark."

"Who—what were those?" I trembled, thinking the worst. She was still here, she was strong and she left that book for me to follow, I chanted to myself.

"Could you not tell they were bones? A skeleton one could call it," he said.

"I'm aware," I said sharply. "But who's."

He looked at me strangely and let his head hang, his body leaning against a covered staff he held in his hand. It was almost as tall as him and his sickly pale skin matched a silver moon. His face was harsh lines and misery entwined.

"You sound scared, what exactly are you looking for?"

I wiped my tears away. "How do you know I'm looking for something?"

"Every fresh blooded human that steps inside the body of the woods is looking for something. It could be anything. Love, hate, riches–"

"I'm looking for my mother," I told him.

Recognition clouded his face but only for a second before it became pained again as new blood trickled down his hand.

"I see. Maybe that was her?" he offered.

Fury ignited me as though I'd been struck by the catholic God.

"Of course they're not hers!" The man looked hurt from my words or maybe from whatever had ravaged him here. I could not decide.

"She's not dead. This place it—it's not death it's…something else. This place is for the lost, not for those who seek death."

"Humans don't reside here. They only pass through. Some can be stuck but…they don't become anything more than mute skins.

"How do I know you aren't just lying. It said you couldn't, in the book. But you play your words as tricks."

"A book?" He sneered. "That is what you know of this place?"

"How else was I to find it?"

"It's for the lost. This place finds them. Their pleas are heard because they are desperate. The only sound of humans we know from here. And the forest answers."

"Well my mother was desperate. She wanted to escape and I just want to be with her."

"Is that all?"

I nodded.

"And what would you be willing to give in order to do that?"

I saw the way his teeth were sharper than my own, the way he reminded me of some great evil in the book of fae. What would he know of my salvation?

"Anything," I said. I gripped my hand tightly, trying to stop its shaking.

"There will be many who will tell you lies but I can only tell a truth, as the light shines on things hidden, like secrets," he said. "If your mother has not come back, I fear she may be gone. You shouldn't be out here anyway. Darkness is never ending tonight, it isn't safe for the weak," he said as though we'd shared a friendship.

I stood quickly, almost swirling myself unconscious. My breathing rapid, I screamed again, "Mother!"

"Shhh!" he scolded. "They'll appear if you don't quiet."

"Why should I listen to you? You're nothing but a walking corpse."

I looked through the thick shadowed branches that felt suffocating when he said, "I was once a king, only now I've fallen from my high seat."

I looked at him. The stained cloak, the staff that wasn't a sword.

"You are no royal thing. If you were, you would've seen her, heard her," I said.

He coughed again. His blood splattered onto a tree. Which contorted like a corpse corroding and then breaking each limb. A slick of bright gold sheened upon it, and small white flowers grew from the low branch. His blood dripped to the ground making a small puddle beneath him. He could be considered handsome if he scrubbed himself and could possibly possess charming honor if he hadn't been standing so diffidently.

"Let me show you."

He limped forward and lifted his hand to the open air in front of him. In one smooth motion, light poured into the forest. Its buttery decadence enveloped the woods in a false warmth and left it just as quickly. It almost brought tears to my eyes as it vanished.

I gasped, "What was that?"

"Life. Everything it needs to breathe. I am the Oak King, one of light and Spring. Ender of darkness and all it holds hostage."

I slowly shook my head. "That can't be. The Oak King was pictured as a tall greenish man in flowered gold. Look at you."

"I told you I had fallen from favor for a time."

My heart raced at the opportunity. I almost forgot my courtesies and gently smiled.

"If you are what you say, a king, then you can bring me my mother. You should know all your subjects in this forest then."

"I no longer rule it. Besides all that, I know the truth as I know a blue sky, and your mother is gone. Yet there may be purpose, accept my hand, bind yourself in lovely I dos to me and I can grant anything for a wife. We can bury your deceased and let the light shine on her grave to start my long reign." He offered his hand.

I thought of my father's laughter, albeit drunken and the memory of my sister's twisting each other's hair into braids.

I remained staring at his hand when the ground began to thump, dead trees glowing began to shake. Something was coming. My breath quickened. A horde of gallant black steeds blew in from the open woods, carrying giant knights in brown and black silk. Circling us, the Oak King dropped his open hand and stood sheepishly behind me, the aroma of dead lilies suffocating me.

The largest horse, holding the largest man with a giant crown on top of his head, stopped the gallop.

"I hear we are offering our hands of marriage on this day, Oak," the man said. He jumped down from his horse, and misted shadow followed with him, trailing his cloak like spirited crumbs.

The Oak King scurried back, as quick as his moldering body let him. I stood still as darkness did not frighten me well enough.

"And you must be Bridgette, are you not?" the man with the crown said. "Your name has echoed through the trees. It is not so often that we still receive humans." He offered a slight bow that brought his head no closer to mine, as he towered over all.

As unfrightened as I was, I stood entirely still with my mouth slightly agape. The drawings depicting these kings of seasons hadn't been close enough to the sheer awe of seeing them up close.

"I would hope to bring all my subjects to the night's celebration, and bask in this one's victory. My reign shall continue and prosper for all to bear witness."

"I haven't come to bask in anything other than my mother's presence. You must know where she is if you rule over these woods. She came here last Solstice, she would have looked just like me," I pleaded.

The Holly King remained slightly vexed but still held his shadowed arrogance in vague hubris. I almost threw myself to my knees to beg him for her.

When they said they couldn't find her, my sisters wept for days until the snow soon melted and gave way to spring. Drying their tears, while mine remained frozen. I imagined her every night, seeing her amongst these creatures in a warm darkness, more peaceful than she'd ever known.

"Did you not see her?" I pressed.

"I believe I did. Your beautiful mother shares such a face with you," he said. "Don't you remember Oak? Or do you forget you made to send her away, back to mortal lands."

I peered at the Oak King. He gathered himself slightly and raised his head.

"I only told her what she needed, not what she wanted."

"What she wanted was important," I said to Oak.

"And she was smart enough to come with me," said the Holly King.

The Oak King stepped towards me despite how weak he seemed to become near the Holly King. "But she should've gone back to you and your family. You all could have helped her."

"My father couldn't help a flower from wilting even in a great big garden. He was no use to my mother's pain nor mine," I declared.

The Holly King placed a hand on my shoulder. "Light can bring such a glaring irritation to one's soul but the night can be a comfort. Marry I, instead of a dead man, and I can give exactly what you desire. Your mother."

The Oak King grabbed the arm of my dress, his grip ripping the button off the cuff. "I can offer you a burial. A proper solstice sleep for her. Years ago, they would bury their royal and when the sun rose, it shown onto their grave in stunning light. Letting it guide them to rest."

The Holly King snickered behind her. "That is a horrible offer, you have become desperate in your pursuit to defeat me, but none will prosper. You couldn't make a flower grow let alone find the girl's mother."

The Oak King looked back at me. "But neither can he. He will only imbue the past to your current eyes, and blind you with the memory of her. It will not be her, and she cannot rest until you face the truth. Your mother is gone."

Irritation laced my body in a tight corset, and I wanted to rip the damn thing off with claws.

Why had he been so feverishly denouncing my hope as though I were only a foolish child. Oh, how it ignited such an anger I haven't known since I'd been one.

"He lies. He is old and graying, can't you see? His green is faded, and this is my longest night yet, may it reign forever. Your mother sits in my kingdom. Marry me, and only then can my power be extended to you."

His voice was buttery and gentle and none of the croaking, begging the Oak King had done. One was desperate, one was fruitful. And I could not follow both. I could stay here forever, and let the darkness eat me alive and join her. *Let it reign forever.* I looked at the Oak King. A part of me thought he was telling the truth, but whose? It sounded so much like my family. Yet they mourned her like she was just anyone. If they knew her as I did, they couldn't believe her demise. Although what he offered was blatantly unimportant.

I stepped to the Holly King, and he smiled, his teeth were sharply edged, and his jaw was squared, his hair darker than the night sky.

It was exquisitely enchanting to look into the night's eyes and have him grin at you. A smile so much like a friend, but sweeter, softer and gentler.

We walked past the decaying man. The day king, weak and feeble and no use to me, nor I for him. I held tightly to the strong arm of night and followed his horde through the gleaming woods.

His dark castle was a vast open space amongst the trees, with stumps for his knights to sit and a black tree vine decorated throne. Taking my hand, he led me to a smaller seat next to his and continued to hold it as he said, "We must marry at once and bring an end to that Oak bastard! We are to fight at the stroke of midnight, and my knights will prepare for their bout. And you shall wed me in good fortune."

"And you'll show me to my mother."

"That and more, my dear," he said. I yawned, and realized how long I'd been here and how little I'd slept this past year. In an instant, my betrothed's giant arm whisked me out of my seat and guided me gently into rest.

My breath became heavy and oh so labored. My skin was icy and my limbs were stuck. I started to close my eyes, I began to let myself drift. What was this? It felt like a lovely, well-crafted reprieve from living, what was that again? Was it death? It couldn't be, death was final, so brutal. This was so pleasant. The Holly King cradled me using one giant arm, and I let myself be rocked like a child. The king of night smelled like spiced wood and clove. Night was my trail to reverence, and I was following it blindly in awe.

The clement rocking halted in a strange cough, as the King's lungs ushered out smoke and foul, dirtied leaves and foliage, essences of spring.

"When will my mother arrive?" I asked.

"She's already here," he said.

My mother, in her black dress and pale as moonlight, stood in front of the king's seat. She looked younger, she looked happy. I sprang from his hold and held her tightly. I didn't realize I'd begun crying until the streak of water wet the shoulder of her gown.

"I came for you," I said,

She nodded and hummed in agreement. I pulled back as she cradled my cheek.

"Sometimes I thought I'd never see you again, but I knew. I knew I'd find you here. I knew all I had to do was wait," I said, "Right?"

My mother still only smiled and nodded.

"Why aren't you saying anything, I wish to hear your voice again!"

A strained look took her face hostage, and when she opened her mouth, crushed, dead flowers fell to the floor.

When I looked back at the king he only shrugged, "Well I never claimed to be god."

His aggravatingly cavalier attitude towards my watery eyes made for a pinch in my chest that had me like a child again. Lost and uninvolved in the choices of my own life. I wanted to scream at being so misguided.

"You said you'd give her back to me."

"And I did. Is she not standing right in front of you?"

"She's not the same."

"We never are after darkness has touched us. You know that. You've wandered through it, kept me at your side for all the year, and now you're finally with us."

The knights around nodded and muttered in agreement. My face became hot, my eyes swelled. My silent mother made a painful expression, and I looked at her open palms as night swirled in dark mist emanating from her skin. The night was a comfort as it was a terror. The Holly King was only what my nanny had told me as a child, a darkness to drag me down in his misery of night.

I shut my eyes and thought of how long I wasted, dreaming of my own end. How long I could've been mended of my dejected heart, how I devoured my sorrow like it was fresh water from a stream.

Regret sliced my conscience like a sword through a man. In an instant, staring after my hollow mother, my wallowing was not strength nor was it a productive task of myself. Running forward only brought me back to the place I shunned most. The place where my mother was no more.

"She didn't leave me," I said, weakly. I shook my head. "She wouldn't do that."

I choked on my grief as it coated my throat in betrayal.

There was something wrong with me, with us. My life at home was no more than a silent, walking death. I devoured happiness gladly. I could not stand the clutter of life, and every good thing that it attached itself to. But staying like this, in one place, letting the weight of grief drag me to the bottomless pit where winter and night would marry and leave myself in its darkness. This does not honor the dead, it only brings you closer to your own end.

But what would I do? What will I be if not pain? What would I do if not suffer?

I looked up at the sky in vast darkness above me. Here in the woods, there were no stars. No light to be seen, and the moon was covered by thwarting clouds. A gentle breeze wafted over my face. Its suddenness made me flinch. It smelled like peonies and rose. A heaviness strapped my body down as my soul pleaded with my conscience to stand and make itself face the spring's admirable stare. Let it dry my tears and ease my pain.

My mother's fabricated face had a knowing look. Like when you try to cover a spill but of course her maternal instincts know when their child is wrong. When their child must clean up their mess. Holding her hands delicately, I started to draw back. The mist of darkness followed my hands, and a coldness swept over them. My hands became thin and decayed before my eyes. Pieces of skin fell revealing pink flesh stuck on bone.

I gasped and my false mother only raised her brows curiously. She smelled rotten.

I ran. I ran through two knights, and I could hear the thunder of their chase beneath my feet. I was lost and utterly confused when I found my fallen button in a thick layer of dirt. Snatching it from the ground I called, "Oak King! Where are you!"

I spun around, I could smell the dead flowers, he must be here if he has not died yet.

"Oak!" I screamed.

He lay at the foot of a tree, small flowers grew around him but instantly died and withered. I knelt down to him and almost sobbed at the broken sight of him. He had only been trying to help but I'd been too lost in my own night to see it. My mother made her choice. And she decided to leave. She chose the night and followed it gladly, her soul was his now, yet I could still go back to them all.

"Wake up, I need to marry you!" I shook him and the King opened his eyes. They were swirling in dark green, almost black.

The night peaked, and the Oak King groaned. His time was almost up. He would fade, and a world would only ever know night, just as I have this past year. Looking at the Oak King I regretted my haste, my stubbornness. They didn't deserve to feel my pain anymore. I could scarcely punish them as I have done myself. What good has it done? I pulled the king to stand, he was growing weaker by the second.

"Take my hand," he said. And I did. "Do you accept and take my offer of life and light and let my reign begin."

"Y–yes, I do."

The ground shook, horses sounded from afar.

"Ask me, do you take my acceptance as my true nature and desire for life."

They were getting closer.

"Do you take my acceptance as my true nature and desire for life?" I repeated.

"I do," he said.

When I heard their shouts, I kissed the king urgently. Black blood stained my cold lips tasting of bitter gardenia and lilies, and I touched my fingers to it thoughtlessly. I held the look of the king as his face glowed, all paleness ceased, and his skin was brightened green and gold. His cloak's fabric was pure white, and his bones cracked pleasantly as he stood to his full height. He was just as tall as the Holly King now and gold and green looked well on him.

"Your mother is where she was before," he said.

I must have looked scared because he assured me. "She is not as you saw. She is how you remember."

I looked behind me and found the forest had painted itself a vibrant green, starting from the ground and following its way up trees, while moss kissed each rock.

I felt lighter and that same warmth he had shown for only a second when I first met him, grabbed hold of my body again. This time it didn't feel false and I couldn't help my grin.

In the middle there was my mother softly hugged by the patch of silken grass. I was tempted to lay next to her, but I remembered my vows. She'd been here all this time, and she is dead. The only thing kept here was my intense rejection of dull reality. But she was stuck, that's why I couldn't pray for her without feeling a gentle numbness. She couldn't let go, because I couldn't. What a horrid daughter I'd been. I may not ever know why she fled, but I understood the impulse. She couldn't leave until I let her.

I knelt down to her as the chaos began. The Oak King's staff became a long sword and flower knights in green followed him. There were screams of victory. Yet it didn't disrupt the gentle kiss I laid on my mother's forehead as I crossed her arms across her middle. I poured the dirt over her as the soft ground ate her.

And when I was done, the shouting and sounds of clashing metal stopped. When I looked back the woods became bright and alive. Grass and flowers wrapped themselves everywhere and I could hear the morning birds and squirrels eat at the acorns and scurry across bark. The sun touched my face in the tenderness only a mother possessed and roamed to her grave and gleamed across it.

The ground was warm and I thought about my little brother's sweet face and my father and sister's smiles.

Beneath me, grew a bed of peonies and roses.

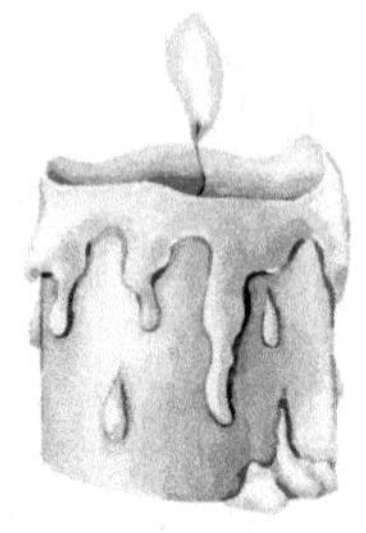

Shadow Work Prompts

*Questions and Exercises to Help
Discover your Shadow Side*

1. What interactions bring out the self-destructive side of you?

2. Do you say or do things for the sole purpose of making someone feel bad? Make a list and think about why you do those things.

3. When you feel isolated or lonely, how do you react? What do you do to manage that feeling?

4. What is something someone said that discouraged you? How did you react to it at the time?

5. List ten things you love about yourself. Explain why you love those things.

6. Name something you really dislike about your past or current self. Why do you dislike it? What would allow you to accept it about yourself?

7. Do you hold onto relationships that you know are unhealthy? What do you gain from those relationships?

8. Is your relationship with your parents the same as it was when you were a child? Are you happy with the way it is?

9.   What does failure mean to you? Are you afraid to fail? Why?

10.   What emotions do you suppress? Why do you think those emotions are so difficult to deal with?

11.   How do you act when you're angry? Are there other ways you can express your anger?

12.   What are your hard boundaries? Are they serving you?

13.   How do you react when people push your boundaries?

14.   What situations trigger you? How do they affect you?

15.   What aspects of yourself would you like to improve? Are these improvements for you or for someone else? Why do you want to improve them?

16.   Do you get jealous or envious of others easily? Can you find a root source of this jealousy?

17.   Write a list of your most favorite traits about yourself.

18.   Do you give yourself the compassion and grace you give others? If not, why?

19.   What emotion are you afraid to feel? Why?

20.   When is a judgment fair and when is it a condemnation of a belief that isn't yours?

21.   What are traits in others that irritate, anger or trigger you? Do you see any of those traits in yourself?

Has someone put a curse on you?

Fill a bowl with water
Get two matches
Put them (unlit) in the bowl, separated
If they remain separated, there is no curse
If the matches touch, someone is trying to curse
you, but it hasn't worked
If they cross, you have a curse on you

The Lamplighter's Daughter

Anne Karppinen

The day is getting darker. The sun has set, and the deep, velvety sky is illuminated only by the smallest sliver of a moon. Shadows stretch out from behind the stones, turning the snow into deeper shades of blue. Trees rattle their branches. There's ice in the air—death too, for those too slow to find shelter. There's a merciless beauty to this weather, something very few people ever get to see, or even know how to look for.

I raise the lantern, trying to cast its glow as far ahead of me as possible. But it's useless. There's nothing to see here, nothing to show. I'd know my way back by the feel of the path beneath my feet and by the smell of smoke from the village. I could make this journey with my eyes closed. There are days when I've done so. The lantern isn't here to guide me or to keep me safe: it serves quite another purpose.

I follow the path down to the village. Houses, their walls prickled with ice, hunch against the darkness, spouting smoke from their chimneys in unison. I can hear pans clanging in the kitchens, plates being scraped, somebody singing a baby to sleep. Water dripping from wet socks over fireplaces. Life going on as life should: mundanely, repetitively, unfurling in slow circles.

Now and then there's a silence. People stop and hear my footsteps. I walk louder than necessary, just to jolt them out of their routines—just to give them a small taste of uncertainty after dinner. Behind a bolted gate, a guard dog bursts into loud barking. I greet it by name, and the dog purses its mouth, confused. It pads over to the doorstep and lies down, a coil of soft fur and pointed ears. Behind the door, people let out a sigh and resume their meal. Now, the dog has a good reason to be on its guard, locked as it is in the dark yard by itself. But the people indoors, with their firelight and bright lamps—why are they so easily startled? Surely they recognise my footfall by now. I walk the same route every day, checking all the lanterns on the way and topping up their oil. I'm beginning to agree with my father: fear can be a delicious thing, if sampled in small quantities and tempered with the feeling of immediate safety.

I make sure to extinguish the lamp before I reach our gate; such brightness feels excessive in our small home. For us, darkness is a relief after a day's toil. It requires nothing of us but silence and rest. In his forgetfulness, father has latched the front door from the inside. I bang on the kitchen shutter, not caring if anyone hears.

"No need to make such a racket." I hear my father's voice through the double doors. As he pushes open the outer one, he adds, "Sometimes I think the gods gave me a son in the shape of a daughter, I really do." He crinkles his hairy face and shuts the door swiftly behind me. "Any luck?"

"No," I reply, stomping snow off my boots.

"But it's not luck, really, is it? The fish, like the signs, arrive just when we need them most." He rests his hand briefly on my shoulder as he squeezes past me in the dim corridor. "You must be hungry."

Father watches me eat. He says he's already had his supper, and I decide to humour him. A grown man knows his own stomach. And, even if our fishing lines will stay empty for the rest of the dark season, we won't starve. The villagers will take care of us: they've always kept their side of the bargain. I glance along the dark walls, at the rows of shelves and hooks with jars and bundles neatly stacked and regularly turned and dusted. My father keeps a clean house—indeed, I've heard them joke in the village that the only thing he ever needed a wife for was bearing me. And I believe they're right.

I don't remember my mother at all. As long as my memory stretches, it's always been my father and myself, taking care of each other. And of the village. Father says that as long as the lore goes, there has always been a Lamplighter living in this cottage. The skill has been passed down generations, usually from father to son. The Lamplighter's task is a straightforward one, and yet something that cannot be taught to an outsider. When I was born, my father knew immediately that I would take over his post one day. He stopped wishing for a son—and started neglecting his wife so that finally she gave up and died. Or that's what I've heard the villagers say.

Although my father has been the Lamplighter for forty years or more, he has taught me nothing. Everything I know about light and dark, the caprices of weather and the changing seasons I've either known all my life, or picked up through careful observation. Ever since I could keep up with him, father has taken me on longer and longer trips on the ice; together we've watched one winter after another arrive, endure, and finally give up under the growing light of the sun.

Now father is saying that I have all the skill it takes to guide the village to the other side of winter

"What happens if I fail?" I asked him once. "Will the sun refuse to come back?"

A vague gesture. "It's not about that. The seasons turn regardless of our efforts. It's about the people: what they need, and what they think they need."

"So you're saying it makes no difference what we do."

"That's not what I'm saying at all. It makes all the difference in the world. A Lamplighter is like the baker. Anyone can make their own bread, and yet we prefer this one person in the village to get up early each morning and sweat at the oven for us. Anyone can walk the winter ice; anyone can raise a lantern to hold back the darkness—and yet most people never will."

"But there's the promise as well," I remind him.

"Yes. The village gave us shelter, in return for our skill. We track the light, count the hours, keep the lamps lit—and they tolerate us."

For we, even after centuries of service, are still outsiders. Anyone who marries into the Lamplighter's family will have to forsake her own. I think my father, in ignoring his wife, made the only right choice. As his firstborn, I'm tolerated here. Any other children would have faced a cruel isolation; having no remarkable skill, they would have had to live out their lives helping their parents—and, finally, me. The one talent that gives reassurance to the village is also seen as an unnatural taint—useful, but ultimately dangerous.

After I've eaten, we talk about my day. Father asks the usual questions about my route, the traps I checked and the tracks I saw, and what the weather was like farther on the ice. How many lanterns had burned out by the time I got back, and how much oil remains in the container. I've fixed these things in my memory while walking, so as to remember even the tiniest of details. I want to prolong this firelit moment, the flicker of the dying flames in the hearth, the soft popping of sparks. Our only safeguard against the pervasive darkness.

But then we know the essence of night, my father and I. Unlike the villagers, we don't waste oil or candles for such simple tasks as eating. The lore says that the Lamplighters carry a bright flame within them, at all times, and that they are immune to the perils of the outside world. I've heard the villagers say that our dreams are of the day, and therefore we're not afraid to close our eyes against the approaching night.

I don't know what other people dream of, in their bright bedchambers, under the oppressive eiderdown. I've heard my father whimpering in his sleep, but haven't dared to ask him what he sees. My own dreams are mainly of ice and rock—of cold things and hard things. Things that have no yearnings. Yet, there are nights when I cannot sleep for the scorching flame inside me.

⟐

The day begins at sunrise. In winter, when the working hours are few, there's a feverish bustle in the streets from the earliest dawn to the falling of dusk. I'm often awakened by the sound of clanging metal or breaking ice, or else to the shrieks of children who chase each other out of doors, burning pent-up energy. Father is always up before me, swearing at the stove or at his damp socks. Neither of us are creatures of the first light;

71

inner light or no, it takes some time to get us reconciled to the new day.

There's usually something fresh for breakfast: a piping-hot loaf, a liver pie, or silver-sided fish straight from the sea. Morning is the best time, food-wise. Father says that's because the folk still remember the terror of the night before, and are more apt to remember us as well. It used to worry me that some day the villagers might forget about us altogether, or that they would find someone else to banish the night for them. Neither of us are well adapted to the endless requirements of domestic life. Father would rather go about shirtless than to pick up a darning needle. I have no idea how to milk a goat or grow a turnip. Whatever we need, our neighbours are happy to provide.

Lately a new kind of fear has begun to haunt me. I'm not afraid of the fickleness of folk anymore; I know that ours is a rare breed and the chances of another one wandering into the village are remote. Father seems sure of my gift: otherwise he would never send me out into the darkness alone. I, on the other hand, am not so sure anymore. Some days I walk and walk along the familiar routes, and cannot remember what I'm supposed to be looking for. I stand there, listening to the wind howling against the ice, and slowly begin to lose my grip. I long to be blown apart, to be mingled with the white oblivion of the longest season, just to feel some other essence against mine.

Yesterday I heard voices on the wind. Human or animal I couldn't tell, but my first impulse was to run towards them. Not with a harpoon in hand, but open-armed and curious. This of course is the first sign of mid-winter madness. Nothing good ever comes from the outside, I've been told: all who speak a different tongue or wear a different cut of clothes should be shunned, if not shot on sight. Although the villagers take care of each other readily, all possessions are jealously guarded against intruders. In this harsh world there just isn't enough to go round. Yet to me it seems that the light and warmth of a fireplace can be shared with a dozen people, just as easily as with two.

I think father agrees. I'd like to ask him, but lately he's begun to turn inwards. He studies his face in the darkness of a window as if he doesn't recognise his own reflection. Some days he calls me by my mother's name. The worst days are those when he refuses to get out of bed and just stares at the ceiling, unhearing and unspeaking. After a day like that, the only thing I can do is to walk as far as I can, and lean towards the foreign voices on the ice.

☧

For three weeks now I've come home empty-handed. The villagers go on with their lives behind their shut doors at night, hoping that the blizzards will sweep the winter away in their wake. They'll be needing a sign soon. Something that says it's safe to walk abroad again; that there's no need to fear the winter night that chills the blood in their veins and brings unseen dangers to their doorstep. That the seals and whales are coming for the brief season of breeding and bloodshed. I should be looking for that sign, scouring the ice-covered vastness for it—on my hands and knees if necessary. At night, I should be questing out with my mind, or dreaming of bright things to come.

But that's not what I do. Each day takes me farther from the village, away from the complacent circle of the island. I walk in a straight line until I'm exhausted, hoping for the darkness to overtake me. Yet every time

I turn back before the light fails and find my way unerringly home. Like a bird returning, I have my compass set for life.

Today, as I make my way south, I see the dark shapes of swans on the horizon: the first migrants are on their way to their summer homes. Somewhere, the ice has started to melt; cracks are appearing in the uniform surface. Soon, the bridge that connects us with the dangers of the outside world will be broken, and the village will be safe again for the warm, light months. During the summer, the sea currents will lead astray anyone who tries to navigate north.

I know then what I must do. It must be soon. The nights are still cold enough, and spring always has a few storms in store. On foot, it'll take me days to get to the next island. The half-remembered wisdom of our people says that even by boat the way is long and difficult. This is of course why they chose our island in the first place. No one gets here, and no one leaves. The people living here see the first light of the coming summer: they have the guidance of the Lamplighter and the long lore that goes with it.

The swans are a sign enough, whether I'll be here to report their return or no. The sun will make its inevitable circuit; birds and seals will find their nesting-places and grass will push its way out of the warming earth. If the villagers want reassurance, they'll have to venture out to the ice to look for it themselves. If they want light, they'll have to learn to keep their own lamps burning.

At night, as soon as father has fallen asleep, I start packing a small bag. I don't have a lot of possessions to begin with, and I don't really know what I'll need on my journey or after it. I'd like to take some of this familiar darkness with me. I'd like to take the soft sound of my father breathing. He told me today he won't live to see the summer. I think he knows my plans, and approves. He knows that even a fast promise of five hundred years' standing has to be broken someday.

Father says that a Lamplighter only sees a small way ahead, but within his circle of light everything is safe and certain. The flame I carry grows brighter by the day. I fear that if I keep it trapped, it will eventually burn me alive.

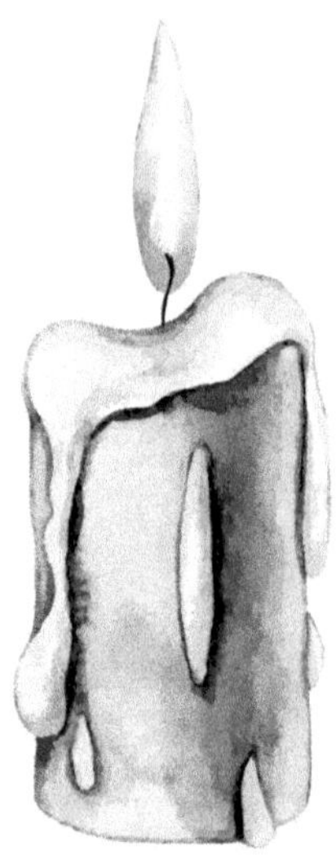

His Return

Jan Cronos

Widowed,
brown velvet frock,
her pale drawn face.

The creaking sound-his old rocking chair.
Her sob in the absence of light-
a power failure.

On the windowsill,
white plastic menorah-
nine electric bulbs

unlit.

A figure, phosphorescent
in darkness.

In its translucent hand,
a single match.
A flare, the scent of sulfur.

Hanukah candles burning bright.

New Year's Day Cleanse

Throw Bay leaves, Rosemary, Thyme and Cinnamon into a pot of water on the stove and let it simmer.

Sprinkle Sea Salt on the floor with the front door. After about an hour on the stove, take the pot off and move from room to room, letting the fragrant steam waft into corners. Put back on stove as needed.

Clear each room this way, imagining the fragrant steam as light. You may say whatever words you wish to indicate you are clearing the house of old stagnant energy and welcoming in bright new light energy.

Finally open the front door, steam the entrance room. Then sweep the salt out.

Lastly, hang or tuck a cinnamon stick at your entry way and discard the water and herbs in your front garden.

The Hunting of Tulikettu

Jordan Bianchi

"When you see your chance do not forsake it, for it may never return."

Grandmother's parting words haunted every step of Veikko's hunting trip.

Days ago he had left his village to kill a great beast on his own and prove his worth as a man.

High in the northern lands, it was the time of the polar night. The sun had not risen above the horizon as he ventured through the forest, and it would not rise for several weeks.

He had tracked a bear and followed it along the river. He readied his bow, but before he could take his shot, another appeared: a challenger. The bears wrestled, teeth barred and claws drawn. It was a vicious battle. A nearby tree fell victim. In time, his bear, wounded but still alive, was once again alone.

Veikko drew back the string of his bow.

Grandmother had helped him split and smooth birch trees, cut feathers and adhere them to the smoothed wood with glue from rabbit skin. The village's arrowsmith supplied him with arrowheads for his hunt. Every hunter was given the same amount before they left on their journey: ten.

Veikko's quiver now held just one arrow. One had pierced the shoulder of a moose but did not bring it down. Another made a reindeer stumble before it dashed away and vanished into the night. Many had broken upon impact with trees or rocks. Many were lost somewhere in the wilderness behind him, concealed by the snow.

This one had to make its mark.

The bear stood up on its hind legs to eat berries from a bush.

Aim was not Veikko's strong suit. Neither was timing, as his family always reminded him. All he had to do was strike below its shoulder, and he would pierce its heart. Nothing more. Nothing less. The other men had done this. To win his village's respect, and the hand of Sigrit, the woman he loved, he had no choice.

With shaking hands, he released the arrow.

It flew through the needles of a fir tree and pierced the ground beside the bush. The bear did not look up from its meal.

Veikko was dismayed. He wanted to try again. The arrow looked unbroken, but he would have to wait to collect it until the bear moved on.

He fumed at the bear as it took its time savoring the berry patch. Had it really not seen the arrow at all? Was it teasing him with its apparent lack of fear?

Snow fell. The quiet of arctic night continued unbroken. After some time, the bear finished its meal and went on its way.

With a yank, Veikko retrieved the arrow. The arrowhead and wood were intact.

A second chance.

He had no food left so he ate the berries the bear had passed over. They were tangy and sweet. He put some in his bag. He wanted to follow the bear, but it was nowhere in sight. Its tracks were filled in with fresh snow.

Veikko's stomach grumbled. He would have to fish again soon so he could survive until he took down a formidable creature and returned home with honor. Although, he was losing faith that that would happen after all.

Defeated, he retreated to his tent by the lake.

The snowfall stopped. The sky cleared.

He heard something by the water. He crept down, as quietly as he could, and looked through the thicket of hibernating vegetation that ringed the frozen lake.

Veikko's heart skipped a beat.

Circling around the fishing hole Veikko had chiseled the day before was a polar fox. It appeared to be following a fish with its clever eyes.

But this fox was unlike any other he had seen trying to steal food from his camp. An iridescent kaleidoscope of color glowed outward from the fox's body to the tips of its fur. They flickered and breathed like flames of his campfire.

Grandmother had told legends about this fox since he was a child. But no one had seen it in hundreds of years.

This was Tulikettu. Its tail twinkled with the same flames that created revontulet, the fox fires, the ripples and ribbons of ghostly, magical light that sometimes flickered through the northern skies.

This was his moment. Missing the bear had given him a second chance. Sirgit would undoubtedly choose him if he brought back the pelt of this magic fox.

Although Veikko thought he had not made a sound, the fox turned to look at him with eyes as dark and endless as night itself. It watched Veikko curiously as he approached. Its furs flickered in time with its breaths.

Veikko raised his bow.

As he pulled back the notched arrow, he felt the weight of the bow, the weight of his family.

Veikko set his aim between the fox's galactic eyes. His arm shook. How could honor be won by the death of such a creature? The energy of the heavens emanated out from its pelt. He lost himself in its eyes, twin stars that were wrapped in arcs of colored light.

With a heavy sigh, he lowered his bow. He tucked the final arrow back in its quiver.

Grandmother would be beside herself if she knew such a creature had been spared. In her stories, wealth and fame were said to be bestowed upon those who captured Tulikettu. But he could not bring himself to do it. It was wrong.

Tulikettu lowered its shoulders and bowed its head with unmistakable kinship. Somehow Veikko knew it to be true. It curled its glowing tail to its snout, and with a quick tug from its teeth, plucked out a clump of twinkling furs. It gently placed them at Veikko's feet.

Then it shot across the frozen lake like a shooting star. As it ran, colors of the rainbow — green, pink, blue — sparked off its flaming, iridescent tail and lifted off into the sky, higher and higher, until they burst into radiant curtains of revontulet. The display grew longer with each leap of Tulikettu's paws. Its tail streaked flames across the entire night sky like a painter's brush against a blank canvas.

Before long, the fox disappeared beyond the horizon. The Northern Lights were all that remained of the encounter. The Lights, and the strands of magical fur.

Veikko stooped to examine the gift given to him by the fox. On the snowy ground, the furs flickered like coals nipped by a fresh breath of air.

At his touch, they were neither warm nor cold. A murmur of shimmering light shone from within the furs. He stored them in his bag before the wind stole them away.

Although he had not made a kill, he was cold and tired. It was time to go home.

Grandmother stood alone at the edge of the village, silhouetted by the dancing sky lights. Veikko, defeated and spent, could barely look at her. Wordlessly, he opened his pack and took out the twinkling furs.

"You met Tulikettu," Grandmother whispered.

Veikko nodded. Grandmother led Veikko to the great fire at the center of their village. Veikko hung his head low. "Veikko has shown great courage on his hunt," Grandmother announced. Veikko was confused. The villagers were puzzled as well. Veikko bore no pelt or head. But when he opened his hand, they too were enchanted by the sight of the glowing strands of fox fur.

Grandmother took the flickering furs and wrapped them around the head of his final arrow. She lifted it high into the air and walked around the fire. Sparks flicked off the furs and fresh ribbons of revontulet burst out and danced overhead.

"You did not forsake yourself by letting the fox live. You are the reason we have light in the dark," Grandmother told him. "This gift is greater than any that death could bring."

The villagers, all his friends and neighbors, congratulated him. They were spellbound by the sight above.

Veikko fell under the spell of Sigrit's beauty as she walked toward him. His face flushed as red as the curtains of revontulet as she took his hands into her own.

The villagers began to play music and to dance and sing. Sigrit and Veikko danced under the Northern Lights. Together, they celebrated Veikko and his gift from Tulikettu, knowing that forevermore, his furs would illuminate the depths of their endless polar nights.

Little Wishes

Write your wish into the wax of a candle before you burn it

Whisper your wish into a bay leaf before you cook with it

Write your wish on a glass bottle with a lid. Fill it with water, and put it out under the full moon for an hour. Then drink the water

Wash your hands with salt and cinnamon on a full moon night for abundance.

The Wishes of Eirlys

Enid Paige

In midwinter, the goats are milked by lantern light. More trustworthy than cows, they're wise enough to aim their kicks beyond the flame. Olwen is forgiven her kicks on account of being surly and old and my favorite. The delivery of twins this spring and my recent pleas have saved her, but someone will be roasted tonight.

There isn't much that's sacred in the cold months, for a poor man nor a chieftain, like my father. Even the proud apples shrink to leather, pretty crones in red wrinkled rows on the cellar shelves. I loathe winter. My mother had a cruel heart, naming me Eirlys when she birthed me during a solstice snow storm. That's why she died. Not the bitter heart, but the bitter cold.

I started leaving the notes, folded in the shape of a star, on my eighth birthday. An iced cake and a prayer. *Take me away, I shall never ask to return. They won't miss me for long. I won't miss them at all.*

I am glad to be the youngest. Dispensable. My sisters were just glad when I was old enough not to need watching. My father is buried under too much grief to care about anything more than accepting the yearly tithe. His silence says how much he wishes it had been me instead of mother.

The suitors came, one by one, raising barns and building fences and accepting a chieftain's daughter's dowry in return. Before long, I was the last. No one is left to celebrate my nineteenth birthday with me. My mind turns once again to freedom. Eleven winters. Eleven winters, I have wished to be free of this place. I can wait no longer.

My father slaughters the goat as I light the candles, and together we pray and pray for an end to the darkness. If it is a different darkness we seek deliverance from, perhaps there is a way we can both be satisfied. When I am gone, so too his talisman of loss. I secret away cakes and mead and supplies in a bundle as he lights the Yule log. I know it won't be long before he's snoring by the fire. Then I will take my leave.

The waiting is interminable. Though I am frog-throated, he insists I sing. I permit him this last sacrifice, my will unto his, and I sing. I call for the dawn and long days of summer, may they warm him in a way I never could. I summon flourishing fields and fat sheep and rich milk and wish it all upon him. For myself, I sing only a single song. In the time of rest, make ready for great change.

Finally, his arms are heavy with mead and sleep, and I slip away into the frigid night. Some time during our prayers and song, it started snowing. My footprints from the barn are merely shadows under the snow. In an hour they will be lost. I walk backward, shoving my heels down to leave good impressions. If I'm lucky, he will believe them to be my egress from the barn to the warmth of our home. His home, no longer mine. It never really was.

Behind the barn, I shift to a shuffle. I sweep messy swaths of snow into incongruent humps as I make my way to the trees. I'll leave no trail for him to follow, for I am bound for another world.

Within the shelter of the forest, the snow and wind fall away. I am no fool. I grip a sharp knife in my fist and make quiet steps. The hard light of the moon on the snow was enough to see by, but under the canopy, I am joined by shadows. The deep silence of sheltered animals and dying winds is all around me. Only the sound of my own labored breathing is in my ears as I hike as far away from my father's farm as my legs will carry me. I walk for what I'm sure is hours.

When I reach the oldest part of the forest, I select a giant evergreen and make my camp beneath it. With gloved hands, I scrape out a space in front of me and build a fire. Before I settle down, I hang my mother's golden necklace on a branch overhead as a beacon, as a gift, as a dowry. I eat an iced cake and sip at the jug of mead, reserving half. I set another cake out on a stolen gold plate. It stings to think my father will miss that more than his own daughter, but I have no illusions to the contrary. I pitch holly berries into the fire, one by one. With each, I cast my wish. *Come for me. Take me away.* I add logs to the fire and watch for signs of dawn.

Despite my stubborn efforts, I cannot outrun sleep. When I wake to the sound of bells, bright morning light stings my eyes. I wiggle my toes. No frostbite, then. That's good. It was foolish to allow myself to fall asleep in the snowy woods. If not for the metallic jingle, I may have never woken at all.

The glare in my eyes recedes as the crunch of footsteps nears. I pat the ground and find my knife beneath my skirts. Only then do I lift my gaze.

It is not my father, nor any other common farmer. I can tell by his boots that he is a prince. "There you are." He smiles at me as if we are already lovers.

"Here I am." I tip my chin boldly. I did not come all this way to shy from my destiny now. My prayers have finally been answered.

"You're bold. I like that." He does not shy away from destiny either. His fearsome green eyes assess me. Whatever he finds, he must approve, for he nods and extends a hand to me. "I got your letters."

"My letters?"

"Ten of them. Last winter, when the gates were opened, I came. I saw you, and I could not look away. I went that night to my mother and asked of her a boon. I was meant to marry a princess of my kind, but I told her I had met with a princess most fair and asked what I could do to break the engagement with another and make you mine. She said I must go to the king who was my intended's father and ask how I may repair the slight between our kingdoms. He gave me many tasks, and I completed them all joyfully, for a chance to win your hand."

A question forces itself past my lips. "What am I to an elven princess?"

"You are bold, and true. You are diligent and do not accept impossible as an answer. You did not surrender hope." He pulls me to my feet, and I fish for some response to his declaration. While I had hoped and hoped, I had not been sure that my pleas would be heard. And yet, here he is. I can only hope he is not too good to be true, and resolve to find out for myself.

At a loss for words, I resort to fine manners. "Would you share a drink with me? I am sure you've come a long way."

"I travel at the speed of thought. But I will accept your offering with thanks. Please, sit." He waves his hand, and my camp becomes a feast table. It is absurdly long for the two chairs at the head. Laden with jugs of mead and ale, breads and candied fruits, and the most ponderous stuffed goose. Its jeweled platter exceeds the table's width to hang over the edges, dripping fat into the snow in a steady drum beat.

He pulls my chair and fills our cups. I finally know what I want to say. "Will you tell me about your tasks?"

"Many tasks did the king bid me undertake." The prince sips his wine, then begins laying our plates. Each item he lifts before me, that I may choose what pleases me. "The first was to compose a song to make him weep, with only the accompaniment of a dozen drummers. He thought to drown out my words, but my voice is strong and true. As is my love for you." He pauses to look me over as he passes the plate. "Your teeth are chattering."

He waves his hand once more, and I am swathed in a fur-lined cloak with boots to match the finery of his own. I offer my thanks, but he waves it away. "You are welcome to anything I can give. Now, the other tasks. Next came the king's order to assemble before him eleven pipers who could carry the same tune. In my homeland, each piper whittles his own pipe, and so they are rarely just the same. However, the king did not know that my sense of pitch is strong and true. As is my love for you."

"Again, he set me to a task. This time, he bid me find ten men who could leap over the top of his great keep and land upon their feet. His castle is the grandest in our lands, but I sought out the greatest athletes and saw them trained until they could clear the height. My determination is strong. As is my love for you."

"His next task for me seemed simple at first. Find nine ladies willing to dance in his court. Dancing is a forgotten art where I come from, but I studied the ways of your world and learned a dance. I taught them myself, for my sense of duty is strong. As is my love for you."

He fills our cups with mead once more and raises a knife to carve the goose. Looking at me, he lets his hand drop, the task forgotten. "Your eyes shine like jewels. And though none can do them justice, I would like to try." He lifts empty hands and places them over mine. My wrists and fingers become heavy with stones and gold. He raises his eyes to my neck. "May I?" At my nod, he leans forward to rest his lips against my pulse, adorning me with a necklace of fire opals.

He tells me about the next tasks. Eight maids to milk his unmilkable cows. With wit, he sought out goat keepers, whose small hands fit neatly round the udders of the king's intractable kine and coaxed milk into the buckets. Seven swans he caught, his feet as light as wings on the water. The king's six geese had let their nests go fallow, but my prince crafted for them a bower of such loveliness that they released eggs both through the summer and winter.

"I hope my home pleases you. It is built of white stone in a land of ice, but I swear you will never suffer the cold. I have never met a problem without solving it, and more than that would I do for you. My castle is known for its grand fires. The king knew this when he set me the next task. I was to bring him five rings of fire that could never be extinguished. I crafted him a sculpture for his garden, made of five interconnected golden rings, their centers encrusted with rubies so that they would burn in the sun and cast their glow into his throne room. Fire can be fickle. So unlike my love for you."

"But how can you say that this is true, especially after telling me how you spurned your betrothed?" I ask, although I admit to myself that I feel an overwhelming bond with him already. It is as if I have loved him all my blind human life, and only recently been given the gift of sight. I know that every plea I sent was for his ears alone. And now, I know that he was listening for me.

"She was never meant for me. You are." He lifts his shoulders. Finally, he carves the goose. Succulent slices of tender meat he piles on my plate, followed by plum and apple stuffing. I wonder how much of this softness I feel for him is from the drink as he refills my glass a third time.

"Perhaps when I finish my tale, you will understand. By this time, I had completed eight tasks, and had no idea how many more he would enforce upon me before permitting me my freedom from a pledge made by my mother when I was only a child. I was resolved to do all he asked, for I knew my true destiny lay beyond them. And so I took on the ninth task: bring before the king four birds who knew his name. In my lands, no such thing exists. Birds can be lovely minstrels, but words are beyond them. In your human lands, far from here, birds with powers of speech can be found. Four of these did I train to cry the name of the king. He laughed in surprise, despite himself. I thought then that perhaps my trials were over.

"Instead, he bid me bring three fat hens with enough meat to fill the bellies of his court. Hundreds of them stood in attendance. I saw their smirks as I left to begin my task. Their eyes became large when I presented the king with three massive birds. They towered over me. As does my love for you." My prince lets his eyes drop to the table. A tiny wrinkle forms between his brows.

"I hesitate to call him cruel. He had the best interests of his daughter at heart. But the next task was surely meant to remind me of my broken oath. It was the hardest of them all. He bade me bring him the corpses of a pair of doves. They mate for life, you know." He shook his head sadly. "To kill them would have been an attack on love itself. I could not do it."

"And yet, here you are." I am not silly enough to think the king would release him from his bond with a task unfinished. I know in my heart that he is not the sort to do needless harm. He has a better soul than mine, filled with bitterness toward my parents for deserting me in one way or another.

"And yet, here I am." It is a confession. I bite my tongue and wait for the rest. "There is a witch in the woods beyond my castle. Though she is feared for her power, I knew she could help me. I braved the thorn bushes around her home and begged her to help me find a way to my love that would not poison its innocence. She pricked my finger and from the drops of blood, formed two dead birds. 'The sacred blood of elves is not spilled lightly. You lessen your own life.' I told her that this was acceptable, perhaps even preferable. The better to match you. I find, now that I have the hope of knowing a life with you, I do not wish to meet an eternity you cannot participate in. For what is love, if carried alone?"

I shake my head. I know a love with no one to receive it leaves a body hollow and a heart thin as winter gruel. "You gave much of yourself. I have so little to give in return."

"All I ask is that you come away with me. I care not where, though I confess that I long to see more of your world." My nose wrinkles at the thought of traipsing through the gorse with a prince at my side. I imagine the mud that will ruin our boots. "We could travel the whole of it as we please. I will not forget my promise to take you far from here. I could show you the talking birds."

All I have ever wanted is to go away from this village. I never gave a thought to how far. Just away. I am not opposed to seeing talking birds. I nod.

"Then let me tell you of my final task. Have you had enough to eat?" The feast table dissipates when I say I have. It is replaced by a brazier and a small side table, upon which he sets our glasses, nearly empty. The jug is gone along with the food.

"I came before the king once more. 'A final task, I have for you. If you complete it, I will know your will is true. Though it proves you are a worthy husband for my daughter, it proves also that you are committed to your path. Climb the mountain behind my castle and bring me the golden bird who resides at its peak. I climbed that mountain every day. Camped on its peak through frigid storms, and yet no bird appeared. I was nearly out of hope.

"But one morning, as the sun rose, I chanced upon a great bird, perched on the only tree on the mountainside. It was weak and old, with tattered feathers. It cried most mournful to me, and then it died. I wept, knowing my task was impossible to complete. Without the great bird, the king would not release me from my bond." I grip his hand. His mercy and gentleness pluck at my heart. While I merely sat in attendance of my father's meetings or marched back and forth from the barn every day, he has gone fathoms for our love.

"I wept for hours. Your letters, which I have kept one and all in this pocket above my breast, were my only comfort on that long day. I read them aloud to the fallen creature as the sun set. I poured my every thought into the mourning. And in that dying light, my life was saved. The last glow of the sun struck the snow, and the ruined wings of that ancient bird. Its regal golden body burst into flame. I stood watch until the fire died out. At last, I readied myself to return to the base of the mountain, and my fate. But then, I heard a peep. Turning, I found in the ashes a chick." I cannot contain my gasp. While I know he has found a way to me, I find myself gripped by the same despair he must have felt when the creature perished. With his next words, my heart takes wing.

"It took us all the night to descend the mountain, nothing but a full moon's light to guide us. At first, I kept the chick in my shirt to stay warm. But as we went down the mountain, it grew!" His face is alight with wonder. I do not curtail my smile for him.

"As we neared the base, it struggled out from my breast and soared toward the castle, letting forth a mighty scream. The king and his retinue came running out through the gates to see what made such a thunderous sound. I did not cross back into that courtyard, but laid a single remaining golden feather upon the threshold, taking my leave. And I have since been on my way to you."

I blink, pulling myself from the land of elves back to that of men. My cup and his lay empty on the table. At last, he rises and extends a hand to me. I stare up at him with the only question. As if he can read it in my eyes, he says, "Ask anything you like."

I shake my head, smiling. "You have told me more than enough. But...you have yet to tell me your name."

Now he is the one blinking. "I can give you that. I am called Culhwch. And you are Eirlys. The snowdrop flower. Tell me, Eirlys, are you as eager to begin a new life as I am? If anything I have withheld, ask it now and I will grant it, then let our adventures begin."

I think back on my life, the meager trials I thought I had endured. I find that out of all of it, I am glad to leave everything but one behind. "Olwen. My old goat. If I leave her behind, she will surely become a meal. She is good and noble and too smart for such a fate. Can she come with me?"

"For you, my queen, anything." He waves his hand a final time, and there she stands.

The odd squares of her eyes do not dilate in fear when she beholds my prince. She merely leans down to nibble the toe of his boot. "She likes you already. And so do I."

March

Jean Baur

To sit still
Before spring
And the riot
Of color returns,
To know its coming,
To say to winter
Hang on as long as
You like
Knowing its days are
Numbered,
Knowing we've made it
This far,
Is to trust
The great
Rotating earth
And the sun
That sustains it.

Evergreen

On this March day
I am bundled up
But can already feel
The great freedom
Of bare feet
And air
That kisses my skin.
So although
I'm sitting still
I'm traveling
Forward and back:
My sights on spring
My feet stuck
On frozen ground.

Shadows cannot exist without light.

Author Bios

Maddox Emory Arnold (he/they) is a writer and educator based in Southeast Michigan. His writing explores queerness, gender, mental health, and otherness with a speculative twist, and he particularly enjoys seeking the horrific, surreal, and/or fantastical in mundane spaces and experiences. Maddox's words have appeared in *If There's Anyone Left, HAD, NonBinary Review, Flame Tree Press' Sun Rising Collection*, and elsewhere.

Author of three books, **Jean Baur's** first two books are career books, and her most recent book, "Joy Unleashed: The Story of Bella, the Unlikely Therapy Dog", is in its third printing. Jean has had short stories and poems published in a wide range of literary journals.

Jordan Bianchi (he/him) is a writer and filmmaker based in Buffalo, NY. He loves to write about self-healing, spirituality, and finding one's light through fantasy stories. Jordan is the host of Aurora Airwaves, a podcast about creative recovery, artistic discovery, and how we can take care of ourselves while creating art.

Jan Cronos writes in New York City, USA. This includes poems, flash and hybrids. Recent publications include the San Antonio Review, September, 2024 (Spirit).

Anne Karppinen is a university teacher, musician and writer based in Finland. She holds a PhD in Contemporary Culture, and has been teaching writing - both academic and creative - for over ten years. Her speculative short stories have appeared in a number of publications including *Not One of Us, Impossible Worlds* and *Wyldblood*. Her book, *The Songs of Joni Mitchell*, was published by Routledge.

Jordan King-Lacroix is a Jewish writer from the Blue Mountains, just outside Sydney, Australia. His first book, the non-fiction *Ugly: A Bikie's Life*, was published by Penguin-Random House in 2021, and his short story, "The Last Chosen", in the *Jewish Futures* anthology (Fantastic Books, 2023), was well-received by critics. When not writing, he can be seen gigging around Sydney in his punk band, The Limited.

Jeannie Marschall (she/her/any) is a garden hag from the green centre of Germany who enjoys hikes, foraging, crawling critters, and inventing tall tales with the best of partners. Jeannie mostly writes colourful, queer SFFH stories as well as the occasional poem. Longer works are in the cauldron (ETA 2025).

Enid Paige is a grown-up girl climbing through the window of a fairytale. She hopes never to escape.

Writing for as long as she could remember, **C.L. Roldan** graduated from SUNY purchase and was a student of Screenwriting for 3 years. Now she is an aspiring author of many different genres including fantasy, horror and literary fiction. She loves discovering new ways to tell a story and to share an important message about the human condition that people can relate to.

Sue Westwind is the author of *Lunacy Lost: A Memoir of Green Mental Health* (KDP, 2012), *The Land Erotic: Acres and Ecstasy in Midlife and Beyond* (Say Yes Quickly Books 2022), and *Man Dies, Leaves Widow on Earth: A Cycle of Poems on Intimacy, Nature, and Grief* (Say Yes Quickly Books, 2024). She lives among the wooded hills of northeast Kansas, courting an earth-mystic's path by listening intently to Nature.

Check out the Collections of Utter Speculation
The Lost Colony of Roanoke
The Jersey Devil
Lady in White
The Dancing Plague
Cry Baby Bridge
Upcoming Novella of Utter Speculation:
Pay the Piper by Sarah Connell

And our other Books
Incubate: a horror collection of feminine power
Work in Progress: Story Crafting Notebook
Beach Shorts
Yule
Muse
Grimm Retold

www.speculationpub.com

www.ingramcontent.com/pod-product-compliance
Lightning Source LLC
Chambersburg PA
CBHW071201300726
48975CB00004B/1236